Paraiso

by
Leslie Polit

PublishAmerica
Baltimore

First printing

At the specific preference of the author, PublishAmerica allowed this work to remain exactly as the author intended, verbatim, without editorial input.

This book is a work of fiction. Names, characters, places, and incidents are products of the author's imagination or are used fictitiously. Any resemblance to actual events or locales or persons, living or dead, is entirely coincidental.

ISBN: 1-4241-3043-3
PUBLISHED BY PUBLISHAMERICA, LLLP
www.publishamerica.com
Baltimore

Printed in the United States of America

Dedication:
For Gustavo, who showed me his Ecuador and much of the world
beyond.
He will be in my heart forever.

Palm fronds drop to earth,
Parrots call to darkling skies.
Eternities pass.

Haiku by Richard Rasmussen, 2005

One

Dawn came brightly over the jungle, warming the wet leaves, leaving an aroma like no other…rich, sweet, heady, inviting. With it came the tolling of a bell from the midst of acres of clearing, filled with the mansion, scores of outbuildings and row upon row of low-lying drying racks.

As always, the master was up already; combed, shaven, groomed from waistcoat to laced-up high boots. Don Carlos was the very prototype of what a hacienda-owner should be: serious, responsible and eager to begin another day in his isolated world, away from the cares of the revolutionary aftermath and the constant political bickering in the capital, Quito.

Manabí province was like the name of his property, 'El Paraiso'-'Paradise!' Bountiful in all that makes life worthwhile: from the virgin sands along the Pacific coast to the low-lying mountains above the jungle, were every kind of tropical fruit; trees that yielded precious woods and medicines, ivory nuts, rubber, vegetable wool, cocoa and coffee beans, and fibers for weaving hats and baskets. Indeed, when it was like this pleasant April morning, after the long rainy season, it was another day to thank God for all this abundance!

His mare, Atena, was ready and saddled, lifting her weight from one hoof to another in anticipation of an early morning ride.

Pepín García held her reins loosely, his customary wide grin greeting his boss.

Behind him, workers emerged from several buildings, yawning, stretching and squinting into the already hot sun.

"Buenos días, Don Carlos. Atena is very anxious to get moving! Are you going to inspect 'La Emilia' today?"

"Buenos días, Pepín. No, today I'm going over to 'San Rafael', so I may not be back for breakfast. Please inform Don Eduardo."

"Sí, mi Jefe. I'll tell him as soon as he gets to his office. May you have a good trip!"

Carlos mounted the bay, and with his soft click the mare trotted up the west road toward the plantation of Rafael Gallardo.

Rafael was a good man, but a mediocre farmer, and San Rafael had not been too prosperous for at least six or seven years. Luckily, he didn't have a large family, only one daughter, but he was in need of money that the banks would no longer risk.

Carlos longed to add on the property, contiguous to his own, but Rafael was a proud man and had never responded favorably to hints of annexation. Today, Carlos was resolved to make headway in this matter, and felt that the time was ripe.

María Pilar, the daughter, unlike her plain mother, María Otavia, was a lovely little girl of about seven years. Carlos, himself, at thirty-two, was engaged to marry a Colombian girl, as arranged by his uncle Felipe; and his younger brother by five years, Eduardo, was too old for the child at twenty-seven. A shame!

But there were other incentives, and he was determined to settle the matter once and for all this morning. He would inject much-needed cash into the operation of San Rafael, in exchange for the actual title, with his neighbor to continue the face-saving running of the property.

In addition, he would hint strongly that a marriage into Paraiso was conceivable, as soon as Pilar reached fourteen or fifteen years of age.

As all these possibilities swam in the imagination of Don Carlos, he gave Atena a soft nudge and she broke into a gallop.

Two

Eduardo Castañeda Albán was very like his older brother in appearance: both had sandy hair and blue-gray eyes, but there the family resemblance ended. While Carlos was almost a carbon copy of their late father, Eduardo was very much his mother's son: an Albán, mentally and spiritually.

He was equal to Carlos' resolve and dedication, but there was a sweetness about him, and a strong poetic strain.

This morning, he, too, had arisen at dawn, but stayed by his bedside to say his matin prayers. By the time he was dressed and had descended to the plantation's office, Carlos had gone, leaving only a brief message.

Eduardo could guess at his brother's mission to San Rafael, but was not sympathetic to his plans. They had often discussed adding the smaller property to their own, as the first step in acquiring all the neighboring ones.

He admitted to himself that it was Carlos' drive that made their property the envy of the whole of Manabí. Indeed, their reputation reached as far as Europe, where their cacao was known for its special sweetness and aroma. Just the stamp of "C.C." on their shipments of cacao gave them the highest prices in the world.

His brother was, no doubt, a brilliant, new-age farmer, with a special connection to the land and its fruits that few, if any dueños/hacendados of this region had.

But he, Eduardo, was also gifted as an administrator and monetary executive. El Paraiso was respected in all banking circles, here, and in the capital of Quito. The mere mention of the land's name could bring anything from large loans to special shipping privileges. And the two brothers had done this all alone, building on their family's original land grant from Spain.

Now, on this lovely morning, Eduardo could have relaxed and enjoyed his first café con leche in happiness; but he was not happy. He was already twenty-seven, and still a bachelor who had never been in love. Indeed, between his bookkeeping duties and land inspections, he hardly had time to meet anyone, let alone available young women, isolated as they were on this enormous property.

But, typically, he put personal problems aside and spent the next hour and a half checking the company books and reports from their eight smaller farms' foremen. Just as breakfast time arrived, there was a knock on the door.

Pepín, large hat in brown hand, stood waiting politely as his favorite dueño came to the door.

"Señor Eduardo, can you spare me a moment?"

"Of course, Pepín; come in."

When the two were seated, Eduardo gestured and Pepín began.

"Don Eduardo, as you know, I am married to Graciela Moreno, and now I find that I am to become a father. What we lived on before was enough to get by, but now I will have three mouths to feed, and I will begin to get in debt."

All the workers at El Paraiso were paid every Friday afternoon at Don Ernesto's, the overseer's office. They then had the option of spending their salaries at the hacienda's well-stocked store, or keeping it to spend later in Chone, the nearest town. The latter was a poor choice, since it entailed a long trek of about ten miles, and a burdened return. Few workers had access to a horse or donkey, let alone a wagon.

Thus, the company store thrived, and the peons spent not only their entire salaries there, but became indebted for anything they could not afford. Pepín had managed his stipend well, and was able to live quite comfortably in the free housing provided to all...until this day.

"How much are you making now?" Eduardo was checking a ledger, the original of the copy Ernesto Cucalón kept as overseer.

Eduardo thought, then, of the land practices elsewhere, not sure how much Pepín knew of them. In some parts of Ecuador, small plots of the haciendas' lands were 'given' to the Indians, a captive labor force known as 'huasipungueros'. The natives worked the land with no salary for the right to farm their 'minifundios', or small plots, often having to give back half their crops to the haciendo owners. And many of these peasants were bought and sold with the haciendas.

This had never been a practice on El Paraiso's holdings; they were far ahead of the general social practices of the country.

"Ah, yes, twenty-five sucres a week. Do you think five more would be enough?"

"Well, it would help, Don Eduardo, but I think, with all the new clothes, too, that I could use a bit more, if you please."

"All right, Pepín, we'll make it thirty-five, but that will have to do for at least this year; then we'll see."

He had skirted the land issue deftly, as both were aware.

"Ah, Don Eduardo, you are a generous man, and I am very appreciative. Thank you, señor. Thank you!" and he rose from his chair.

Eduardo saw him to the door, shook hands and went to the opposite side of the office to the door that led to the main house, and passed through it, on the way to a big breakfast.

Three

The grand structure of the family home was built to suit the tropics, to attract the breezes and circulate the humid air blown in from the surrounding jungle. Its windows were generous, long and down to the floor on the lower level, and, like the storey above, topped with wide transoms, to take advantage of cooler mountain air, especially during the humid winter months, or rainy season. On the roof was another low structure, its smaller windows built to match those below, and used to cool the building; as was yet another, even smaller top storey, which was also a bell tower. But its architectural style was nameless: simply the answer to its geophysical surroundings.

The original settlers had, in the late seventeenth century, erected a small edifice to protect themselves from the tropical sun's rays, and all manner of insects and marauding fauna. Then, they were walled in by unfettered growth on all sides, attempting constantly to clear the land, only to find it overgrown again in a matter of weeks. Their home had begun as no more than a large hut, hardly superior to those of the native workers they had displaced and then exploited.

But, as time passed, the property, part of a huge Spanish land grant, was improved when the first Republican Castañeda took it over, and his only brother surrendered his share of the tropical prize in order to join the ranks of other Royalists in the Andean capital of Quito.

Now, in the first years of the young twentieth century, the home building had evolved into an imposing presence, with its generous width and height, in spite of its box-like style.

Carlos and Eduardo kept the family structure and gardens in perfect order, painting the main building every year, sometimes with a new color: now a cool pale blue. The grounds were kept by three talented gardeners, so that the home was surrounded by tall fruit trees and raked pathways that meandered through fragrant flower beds, down to the Garapata river below.

Inside, the home's high ceilings and broad proportions were now comfortably appointed with mostly European furniture that their parents had ordered from abroad. Their two sons, and current owners, now more prosperous than ever, were able to import silverware, linens, porcelain dishware and chandeliers, as well. It was part of Eduardo's job to keep meticulous records of all purchases of the hacienda, and to pass on to the housekeeper the task of counting all of these on a weekly basis.

Eduardo walked through the dining room on his way to the library. His breakfast had been served in a smaller room adjacent to this, where the brothers liked to eat when alone.

Now, as he glanced around, he noted the neatness and cleanliness of his surroundings, and was grateful. At the same time, he was glad of his brother's coming marriage, and felt that the house, though orderly, was somehow 'empty', and that it deserved to have a mistress, and be a home again.

In the living room, a young maid was improperly dusting the ornate oil lamps and wood table tops. He paused to greet her and asked that she go to the kitchen and request of Dela, the head cook, a cup of coffee, to be brought to the library.

The latter was a room dear to the two brothers. It was here that both had studied with a tutor for all their formative years. Using their father's well-rounded collection of the classics, they had mastered some Greek, more Latin, and read all the ancient philosophy and literature. They knew little of North American writings, but read all the great Spanish works, and much of Shakespeare and the English poets in translation.

Eduardo valued this one hour, after his first meal, more than any other of the day. In this peaceful time, he forgot his own life and lived among those of another time and place. Occasionally, inspired by the day's readings, he would jot down a poem of his own, so that many

11

books had small slips of paper jutting out of gold leaves, to be forgotten for many months or years.

His coffee came, on a small tray; and as he sat there this morning, sipping the sweet hot drink, he forgot for a time that his life seemed to be going nowhere, and was bringing him little joy.

Four

"Well, brother, how did your visit work out?"

Eduardo had returned to the office where Carlos appeared at the outside door.

"Come with me to the drying racks, and we'll talk," Carlos answered. Both men were formally dressed, as always, in spite of the now-intense heat. Their heads were covered with pith helmets to ward off the sun.

Pepín and another young Indian, Alonzo, accompanied them, keeping a respectful four or five steps behind their employers. When Carlos gestured, they stepped up to the slotted wooden racks topping a series of long rails that stretched over a large area on one side of the main house.

Slowly and carefully they turned the cacao pulp for the masters to inspect for possible rot. Since the temperature was reaching the maximum for the still mucilage-enveloped cacao beans, they were covered loosely with large green banana leaves. Soon the drying platforms would be pushed into the shaded low sheds at the end of the rails.

Pepín passed one small pile to his employers for inspection, and the workers then backed up and left the two brothers to have a low-pitched, private conversation.

"Gallardo was forced to admit he's in bad straits, so he'll go along with the take-over. I still need his signature, but there's no doubt at all that he'll sign."

While he spoke, Carlos inspected the mound of sweet-sour seeds in his hand, cutting into one of them with his pocket knife, and lowering his face to take in the fragrant aroma.

"They're almost ready—getting redder and sweeter." He took out a handkerchief and wiped his hands.

But Eduardo was thinking of his brother's remarks about the Gallardos. "It will be hard on them."

"There's only one child, a girl—very pretty, and I've already hinted that she can have an education here—with Don Francisco."

"Oh? Well, that's something, I suppose."

"We can't afford to dawdle though; I have to get the other two farms to do the same. We have to expand quickly; the next big harvest begins next month. We need to maximize our advantage this fiscal year—get their crops up to par, and ready for export."

Eduardo thought of 'La Perla' and 'La Cecilia'; small, but carefully tended haciendas to the north and east, edged in turn, on each of their sides by three of Paraiso's eight small farms. Both grew some cacao, but did not have the expertise nor the capital to be big growers; so they relied mainly on the 'forastero' variety—easier to grow and harvest, unlike the Castañedas, who grew the 'criollo' beans. They had, besides, smaller crops of rubber, Brazil nuts, mangoes and other fruits.

Don Felix Huerta and his wife, Mercedes Santos, of 'La Perla', were good people and had no family as yet. Don Alberto Granados, or 'El Grandioso' (The Great One) as he was dubbed by those who resented his grand manner with neighbors and the region in general, had not yet started his family, either, since the master had only recently married Cecilia Montenegro, the only daughter and heir to the proprietor of E.L. Montenegro and Company, a successful import establishment in the growing seaside town of Bahía de Caráquez. Their newly renamed hacienda, 'La Cecilia', was a prize that would be hard, or even impossible, to wrest away.

These thoughts streamed through Eduardo's mind, even as he listened attentively to his brother's remarks on the condition of the latest crop of cacao cherelles or pods.

They had walked over to a shady spot in the garden; a trellised arbor over two benches. The brothers sat down and removed their head gear.

"I suppose old Alberto will be a tough nut to crack," mused Carlos.

"He believes he's the 'Great White Planter of the Century'! We'll have to come up with a good strategy. Can you think of one?"

Carlos counted on his brother's quiet opinions. He was not really a planter, but he, as much as any man in Manabí, understood the running of a prosperous plantation. He was calm and judicious, and meticulous in his dealings with equals and subordinates alike.

"I know time is of the essence, Carlos, but Alberto is a proud man, *and* just married! He can't afford to lose face with his wife and in-laws, or his employees. We'll have to figure out something really convincing!"

Carlos answered in a low tone, as he was wont to do in serious moments. "Yes, yes; but I hear that his crop is not doing well. They really have no idea how to dry it correctly; they still use the old way of burying the seed-pulp in the ground, wrapped in leaves. It's just not as controllable that way!"

"Maybe we can start by offering to take a sample batch of cherelles and dry them here."

"Yes, maybe, we'll see. I think Felix will be more amenable. I could start with 'La Perla' and use it to convince Granados that we're all better off united."

"If anyone can persuade them, it'll be you, hermano."

Eduardo, seldom flustered, rose, stretched slightly and ducked out of the arbor.

"Let's get out of this heat and get some refreshment."

Carlos, frowning with his mental manipulations, followed, and the two strolled back towards the promise of a comfortably cool house, and a short siesta.

Five

The year had passed quickly, bringing both 'La Perla' and 'La Cecilia' under the domination of 'El Paraiso', but Alberto Granados was still farming on his own. All the neighbors, though, had been invited to the wedding, and all had accepted.

Social events such as these were few in this region of isolated properties, and the women, especially, were looking forward to dressing up and visiting with the ladies, and seeing the bride from Colombia.

Eighteen-year-old María Mariana Palacios Uribe, now an orphan, had arrived a week ago with all her family. This included two brothers, Felipe and Alfonso, and a little sister, María Margarita. Her grandfather, General Jorge Luis Palacios, lately a liberal in the "War of 1,000 Days" in Colombia, accompanied her also, as did the primary arranger of the marriage, Uncle Felipe Castañeda.

When Carlos had met his bride-to-be, he was pleasantly surprised. He had not expected this pretty young woman, with her long black hair pulled back in a chignon. She was quiet, but amiable, and had a sweet smile and lovely green eyes. He wondered why she had not married at home, but the men in the family assured him that she had been 'saved' for just such a union as this!

The preparations for the celebration had been started a month before, when small structures had been erected and scattered over the side lawns. Chone's two hotels had sent pastry cooks to live on the property, and the kitchen had new tables to accommodate the visiting staff. Anything that could be made ahead of time was done and stored.

The visitors had been housed easily in several large rooms on the second storey. After their tiring trip of three days from Colombia, they were exhausted, and all had immediately bathed and taken long siestas.

Various young maids had run up and down the large stairway, carrying bundles and cases, hot water, towels and linens. There was a palpable excitement in the air that only visitors from a perceived glamorous outside world can produce in the stagnant atmosphere of the isolated and provincial.

So, much giggling and exchanges of mischievous glances accompanied the girls' trips to satisfy the travelers' every wish and need. El Paraiso was waking up!

Little 'Mara', as Mariana's sister was called, joined in their mirth, and with the reviving energy of an eight-year-old, she joined the help in carrying and distributing the comforts of home to her relatives.

On her last trip up the wide staircase, she concentrated on her load of soaps and brushes, looking only at her feet. Suddenly, a large form blocked her way.

Startled, she looked up into the mustached face of a tall, blond man. "Ah, lo siento, señor. I'm sorry, sir."

The face looked down at her with a smile that allayed her initial fright.

"It's all right, little one. Let me help you."

He took half the load, turned, and changing his direction, continued up the stairs with her.

"So you're María Margarita!"

"Yes sir, I am. But everyone calls me 'Mara'. Are you Don Carlos?"

"Yes, I am. So I'll be your big brother soon."

"Oh! A brother. I *have* two, you know."

"Yes, but when someone marries a sister, *he* becomes a brother, too. Will you like that?"

"Yes, sir. But I won't live here, you know. We're going back to Pasto, in Colombia, after Mariana is married."

"Well, that's sad, but maybe you'll come to visit us. A nice little girl, just your age, is coming from a neighboring hacienda for the wedding.

Her name is Pilar, and you can play together. Will you like that?"
"Oh, yes, please! Nobody is ever *my* age!"
Carlos smiled, and handing over his part of the soaps, patted her golden head, and knocked on the door of his Uncle Felipe.

Six

Carlos waited at his elder guests' door, wondering what to say, since he had just left them, after inquiring as to their comfort. But, since he had assisted little Mara, he had shrugged and come back up, deciding to invite the two men to join him for drinks in the library.

The General appeared at the door, surprised to see Carlos again so soon.

"Si, mi hijo—yes, my son—What can I do for you?!"

Carlos, reddening a little, delivered his invitation.

"That is," he amended, "if you're not too tired."

"Of course, my boy. We'll be glad to accompany you."

So Carlos, the old General and Uncle Felipe descended to the lower storey to have a family conference...

The two hosts had made sure that the bride would have the most comfortable room upstairs. Here, the coolest breezes came through the white gauze curtains, the bed had the best imported mattress they owned, with French linens and bed coverings. All was soft and feminine.

Under a large mirror was a dainty dressing table, and to one side was another table covered with a white embroidered cloth, where an enamel bowl and water pitcher had been placed, along with small hand towels.

A chaise lounge, woven in Jipijapa of the best native export cane, was placed invitingly in one corner.

Now, Mariana stood over her cases and boxes, sorting out her most intimate clothing, and placing small bottles and brushes on the dressing table, while a young maid held dresses ready to be hung.

19

Mara was nowhere to be seen, and she wondered where she had gone.

"Benita, do you think my little sister is all right?"

"Oh, sí señorita. She brought up some soaps, and I think she must have gone back downstairs. There are plenty of people to watch over her!"

"Yes, you're probably right. She's very independent, in any case...Benita, tell me, will it rain tomorrow on my wedding day?"

"No, señorita." Benita blushed and looked away from the new lady, as she was unused to speaking to strangers, especially pretty young ones.

"It's May now, and the dry season is beginning. And it won't be so hot."

"Oh?" replied the Colombian stranger. "And how long will this last?"

"Until November, Ma'am...Shall I hang these dresses on the wall hooks?"

"Yes, thank you, Benita. Careful with *that* one! And then you can go...I'm going to take another little rest."

The girl did a rough curtsey, as the housekeeper, Rosa Mendoza, had shown her, and left quickly.

Downstairs, she joined the other housemaids in the kitchen, who, along with Mara, were being spoiled by the visiting cooks, who gave them little samples of their sweets.

Dela, the head of this realm, smiled indulgently at the noisy group, as she walked about, checking the progress for tonight's dinner and tomorrow's feast. Then, having had enough of their chatter, she shooed them all out into the dining room.

"Run off, then, you little chickens! Make yourselves useful somewhere, but not in here! Better still, go outside and play until supper!"

Laughing, the girls headed out to the lawns, away from possible new tasks, with Mara still tagging along.

Around the corner came the two visiting brothers; sixteen year old Alfonso, and twenty-one year old Felipe; and, again, there was much giggling and whispering from the group, while Mara rushed to hug them.

"Oh, I missed you! Were you napping?!"

"Yes, for a while, but now we're going to explore." Alfonso was already almost as tall as his older brother, and had his same thick brown hair and hazel eyes.

Felipe, though, was now a man, with a new mustache and an athletic build.

"We want to see where the cacao is dried. But we want to be alone! So you can all go and play somewhere else."

The older maids looked taken aback at this thinly veiled order, but joined hands and turned back toward the house, Mara trailing along.

When they had turned the corner, and were unobserved, Benita motioned for all to sit down around her.

"I've seen the wedding dress!" she bragged. "It's so beautiful...all white lace, long puffy sleeves and a high buttoned collar! I hung it up...and it had two or three layers under the skirt!!"

All were enthralled at this first-hand information. And Mara, wanting to be part of the group, volunteered,

"Yes, and she has three strands of real pearls from Spain. They were my mother's; and new satin boots from Bogotá!"

Her audience had never heard of another country but Ecuador, so were unimpressed that something bought anywhere but next door in Chone, or perhaps Bahía de Caráquez, far away at some forty miles west, was worth talking about...

The men, however, were speaking seriously of the late battles of twice-now president, General Eloy Alfaro, to defeat the conservatives of the highlands; the rebellion in their neighborhood of Barbacoas, Colombia; and the rising up, there, of some of their black slaves.

They quoted the latest, now month-old newspapers from Guayaquil to the south, and from the Andean capital of the country, Quito, to the east.

All their faces were slightly flushed from the early afternoon wine, as they were joined by Eduardo, back from a talk with the head overseer, Ernesto Cucalón.

21

After their greetings, Eduardo joined them in another round of claret, and the conversation turned to the impending nuptials.

Uncle Felipe, the diplomat of the family, cleared his throat and began.

"I'm glad María Mariana is resting. It will be a long day tomorrow!"

"Yes, yes," from Carlos.

And from the General, "I'm relieved to find that all is as Felipe described, and that my poor, orphaned granddaughter will be so well taken care of!" He wiped his eyes sincerely as he felt a stab of pain, thinking of his wife, missing her, and knowing how she would have cherished these days; and of their only son, Evaristo, gone now, as well as his wife, leaving their four children in his care.

"Well, sir, please be assured that she *will* be received here with love and respect," from Carlos.

"Yes, General, we will all welcome her and treat her well as the new mistress of this house," put in Eduardo. "And now I believe it's already dinnertime."

At this, they all rose as one, shook hands all around, and followed Carlos out of the room and toward the dining room.

Seven

A breeze ruffled the curtains at Mariana's windows, and as she lay waking, she slowly became conscious of the fact that this was her wedding day. And, it was Sunday! Was she destined to begin her marriage without attending Mass?! She sat upright, now wide awake, aware that this was the beginning of her new life. Alone, far away from her loved and trusted family, she would live with strangers in the midst of a devouring jungle, separated from town, church and friendly neighbors! And she began to weep silently.

A soft knock on her door brought her feet to the woven mat on the floor, and she quickly wiped her eyes and reached for her long peignoir,

"Come in," she called in a muffled tone.,

The door was flung open, and Mara burst in, fully dressed and pink-cheeked with excitement.

"Good morning, my darling sister-bride!"

Mariana smiled, in spite of her sad mood of a few minutes before.

"Buenos días, mi Angelita, my little angel-girl! You can't know how happy I am to see you!" And the sisters embraced warmly.

Mara, though, noticed her sister's slightly sad eyes, and being the child she was, knew that her job was to keep her sister's spirits up.

"Did you know that there's a chapel in the house?! Well, I went there with Don Eduardo this morning. And the priests have arrived from Portoviejo, and Father Juan Bautista is going to live here!" all in one breath.

"Can we go now? Are they going to serve Mass before the wedding? Or, can I go to confession?"

"Yes, yes! That's why I came so early! Hurry, hermana, so we can go before the wedding breakfast! Just wear any dress, "she suggested, as she saw Mariana standing there indecisively.

So, in a few minutes, the two girls descended to the lower level, and Mariana followed her little sister to the 'secret room', which was reached through a hidden door in the library wall.

There, she saw a charming, tiny chapel, with seating for only five or six, facing a beautifully adorned altar, with several native, hand-carved statues of painted wood on either side of a large crucifix.

Both girls knelt to pray in the dim light, and await the priest. Father Juan Bautista entered from another side door opening from the garden, and motioned them toward the small confessional near their seats.

Then, after saying their penance, the two left with the priest by the door which led to a small trellised garden.

The cleric, now able to speak freely, introduced himself, and they sat down on the low benches under the arbor.

"Today is an important one for you, my daughter, and I'm sorry your parents could not be with you! But we all want you to feel welcome; and I, especially, want you to know that I will be living here, for at least a year, and that I will always be available to assist you in any way necessary." He paused, removed his black beret to wipe a bald head, then replaced it.

"Many years ago, our order had two fathers living here, but they were recalled when Don Carlos' parents left this earth. Now, maybe we will be allowed to stay. Los señores dueños…the owners…have had a little house built for me—or us—so I will be close by for your spiritual needs."

He smiled warmly, revealing rather bad teeth, and again wiped his head.

"Now, " he suggested, "I think the señores are awaiting us for a small family breakfast." He rose and, followed by the girls, re-entered the house, this time by another door leading into a hallway.

"Isn't it bad luck for the groom to see the bride before the wedding?" asked Mara knowledgeably. Mariana looked grateful, since she had been too shy to ask such a forward question.

"Well, yes," fumbled the priest, "but here we are in the country, and can't drive to and fro between houses! However, if you wish, you could go up to your room, and I'll see that your breakfast is sent up."

"Oh, yes," agreed Mariana. "You go with Father, Mara." And she quickly turned toward the central staircase and started up.

Unfortunately, Carlos was just on his way down, and the two met halfway.

"Oh, my," blurted the dismayed bride, averting her face, trying not to 'see' the groom.

Carlos was equally embarrassed, and reddened at the unforeseen meeting.

"I'm sorry, I'm sure," he mumbled, lowering his gaze. "Please excuse me......until later...," and he continued downward as fast as possible.

......It was clear that the weather was in tune with a marriage. A bright sun, slightly dimmed by fluffy, scudding clouds, shone over the hacienda, bringing warmth, but no oppressive heat, as more and more guests began to arrive. Approaching the grounds of the house, they could see that earlier arrivals had already tied up horses and carriages along newly cut log fences on either side of the road. Attendants, dressed in their Sunday best, kept watch over their employers' properties.

Neighbors from adjoining lands greeted each other gaily, and soon mixed in with the growing crowd of both strange and familiar faces.

Invitees had come from as far away as Bahía, on the coast, to inland Portoviejo, the capital of Manabí province. Among them, one lone sailor, clothed in the dress whites of chief officer (or mate) of the British merchant marines, walked about, stopping to greet various personages from the banks and shops of his port of call, Bahía de Caráquez.

Among these acquaintances, was the father-in-law of Alberto Granados from 'La Cecilia', José Montenegro. He was the importer of many of the foreign luxuries of El Paraiso, including the new pianoforte from Paris; a rich and influential merchant. He was not

25

overly fond of his only child's husband, but he backed his idea of *not* allowing the Castañeda brothers to take over his farm's cacao production. The father hoped to leave Cecilia his large fortune, especially now that she had one son, and was expecting a second child in a few months.

"How are you, my boy?" he asked of the officer, Joshua Crowley by name. He admired the young Englishman, handsome in his starched uniform, only one step away from captain, at eighteen. He thought fleetingly of his daughter, Cecilia, knowing, ruefully, that it was too late for her.

The two men chatted for a few minutes, Don José admiring the foreigner's fluent Spanish. They were soon joined by a congressman from Portoviejo and another merchant from Bahía. The crowd closed in around this nucleus, and soon Dr. Cueva from Chone and the men from 'La Perla' and 'San Rafael joined them, and were all in excited conversation, mainly political in nature, but also of their crops.

In and out of this group, and others, came white-coated male servants, offering wine to the gentlemen and lemonades to the ladies, who kept apart from the men.

Their conversation was intensely personal. These women had at least a year's catching-up to accomplish in the short time before the actual wedding took place. They noted any changes in physiques, the names of new babies and the possibilities of future gentlemen-callers at their isolated estates.

Even the townswomen, separated from their husbands' daily intercourse with the world outside their sphere of the home, often felt as distant from inventiveness and creativity as their soulmates on the country plantations.

It was just at noon that El Paraiso's bell began to toll, and a hush fell over the now-crowded grounds. All began to gather as near as possible to the trellised wedding arbor.

There, roses had been trained to grow up and over the arch, and wild orchids had been added for scent and color.

Under this stood Don Carlos, formal and elegant in his tail-coat, white tie and striped black trousers, an orchid in his buttonhole.

Soft music of several guitars floated over the guests, when suddenly young Mara, dressed in a filmy rose-colored dress, appeared with a basket filled with every kind of flower from the garden and nearby jungle, some of which she dropped gently on the path before her.

Then, on her grandfather's arm, the bride followed, young and demure in her lacey white gown, its wide skirt trailing behind. The guests, seeing her for the first time, were struck by her quiet and sweet demeanor. Carlos took her hand, and they faced the priest under the arbor.

Their vows were necessarily brief, since the day had grown too warm for a prolonged ceremony. When the father had blessed them and pronounced them man and wife, Carlos bent to kiss the new mistress of his home, and they joined their guests in the shade of algarobo and higueron trees...

Now, Mara was free to play, and was introduced to a little girl from 'San Rafael'.

"So you are Pilar?"

"Yes, and *you* must be Mara."

"I am. I'm eight. How old are you?"

"The same. Let's go over there and talk."

The two smiled simultaneously, and ran to sit in the shade of a mango tree.

Here, the sound of many guests singing the hymn of Manabí with great sentiment, wafted over them.

"Manabí, beautiful land of my dreams...

Where I first saw light...

...your rivers are mirrors

of your smiling country houses and gardens..."

Pilar hummed a little of the well-known tune.

"Where do you live?" asked Mara, not to be interrupted.

"Oh, over there," answered Pilar, and she gestured vaguely to the west, toward 'San Rafael'. "I live in one of those 'smiling country homes'!" she added mischievously.

Mara was charmed by this new acquaintance with the lovely smile

27

and long dark hair. She looked just like one of her dolls.

Pilar, in turn, was fascinated by her new friend: a golden girl, with big blue eyes!

Just as they were about to resume their questions and answers, Mara's two older brothers approached, with several other young men, the British seaman among them.

"Mara!" exclaimed the elder Felipe. "I hope you're not staining your new dress!" At this, Mara jumped up.

"Oh, Felipe, I'm not! Please make the acquaintance of my new friend, Pilar." She turned to her to ask, "What's your family name?"

"Gallardo Díaz," answered Pilar, rising. "María Pilar Gallardo Díaz."

"These are my brothers. The big one is Felipe, and the other is Alfonso. I'm sorry, I don't know the other gentlemen."

Each man in the group stepped forward and introduced himself. The British officer said simply,

"How do you do, young ladies? I am Señor Crowley."

No one shook hands, since it was not considered necessary for two such youngsters—girls, at that!

The small group moved on toward the other guests at the front of the house.

At two o'clock the much anticipated dishes had been served to the guests, seated at long trestle tables, set, as far as possible, in the shade of the largest trees. All the visiting cooks crowded in the doorways, peeking out to see what effect their efforts were making, smiling with relief to see every morsel quickly vanish.

The bride sat quietly with the groom, eating little, her head bent down. Carlos hardly spoke, afraid of embarrassing her. But all around them was noisy conversation and much laughter.

By three-thirty, all seemed to rise on signal, since long distances were to be traveled before nightfall. Those going the forty or so miles to Bahía, or on to Portoviejo, would spend the night with friends or in the hotels of nearby Chone, and start out early the next day for home.

At last, the carriages and horses had all been untied from the new hitching rails, and the roadway was deserted.

Some workers, dressed up today to serve in the garden, still lingered there, dismantling the tables and benches. Others picked up fallen linens and an occasional lost glove, here and there.

But all were tired, and ached to get back to their little houses and families. The señores dueños had gone inside, and there was a slightly sad aura left in the air.

They were unaware of it, but this had been the first, only, of many changes to come to Paraiso.

Eight

Mariana wasn't sure where she should go, upstairs to 'her' room, downstairs with her new husband and brother-in-law who were talking animatedly with her grandfather and brothers in the library, or to the music room where Mara was unsuccessfully poking at the piano keys. She was the bride, but she felt totally superfluous. So she just sat in a far corner and watched Mara pretending to be a musician.

For his part, Carlos was also paying only half-attention to the conversation around him, nodding at the recap of this afternoon's animated topics.

His mind was on this evening's expectations of him. He thought of marriage and grew restless, wanting to find his new wife and be alone with her. Privately, he was glad that business called the General back to Colombia, and that the whole family was to leave tomorrow!

He missed the habitual serenity of Paraiso, and longed to reign there again in the normal tranquility of the place. His brother was almost like a familiar landscape: a tree, or part of the house, who belonged there with him. And now, Mariana, too.

He straightened and focused on his surroundings.

"Gentlemen, please excuse me, but it is late, and I confess to being rather tired. I believe I'll retire. Consider this your home, and enjoy yourselves as late as you wish. Good night."

All eyes were on him as he left the room, not knowing where he could find his bride. Poor little thing; he should never have left her alone!

On top of these thoughts, many came tumbling after. He was alone, in semi-darkness, in his own home, and yet he felt his cheeks flush as he thought of his bachelor history!

Eduardo had always been the quiet one, and seemed to have an inner code that directed him in all his activities. But Carlos, at thirty-three, had not lived such a disciplined life. Outwardly, he was the master of many square kilometers all around him, and of the people who depended on him for their wages and shelter.

But he had inner demons, stronger for having been suppressed. And at times they manifested themselves in deeds he later regretted, and that brought him shame.

Not wanting to sully his lovingly-cared-for daily surroundings, he periodically removed himself physically from them. Eduardo was not the only one who observed his brother on one of his monthly, or bi-monthly trips to Chone. Pepín and the cacao workers also noticed, and would comment among themselves. "The master is going for more provisions!" And there would be a burst of laughter.

Carlos had often been tempted by the younger women of the servants' quarters, voluptuous and carelessly, almost wantonly dressed, in the prime of their lives. But he had thought of his late parents, and the reputation he himself had created of rather severe integrity, and rode instead to Chone, where his activities would blend into a larger populace, where he hoped to go unnoticed.

But Chone was still only a small provincial town, where the inhabitants breathed in and exhaled gossip, So Carlos' 'shopping trips' were often discussed in the most conventional households. Somehow, he was seldom available for an evening's dinner invitation or game of cards, yet he was still in their midst the next day.

Now, Carlos worried that perhaps his habits might affect another, and dreaded bringing disgrace, or worse, to Mariana. He vowed to be faithful to her, if only nothing he had done would hurt her and their marriage.

He was not yet in love, but he felt a real tenderness toward this young girl, now to be left in his sole care, and he quickened his steps, searching for her in every room, automatically following the sound of the piano.

As soon as he came to the doorway, he took in the sad little scene, and determined to rescue this pretty woman.

"Mara," he called, "It's late, and you're going to travel tomorrow. Please go up to your room now, say your prayers and go right to sleep."

Mara, used to getting orders from all the males around her, jumped up, ran to kiss her sister good night, innocently, with no idea of the protocol of this special evening.

"Yes, sir," she half-curtsied, hugged Mariana, and ran to the stairs.

Carlos, taking Mariana's hand, pulled her toward him gently, holding her in a quiet embrace. By now, his former thoughts, added to a very real beauty in his arms, led to an urgency on his part, and he led her upstairs, not to her pristine white room, but to his own, farther down the hallway.

Once inside, he could no longer wait, but began to help a blushing Mariana unbutton her long dress, and then her several layers of undergarments. He was in a frenzy, no longer conscious of her hesitant, embarrassed manner.

With one arm around her, he half lifted, half pushed Mariana toward the wide bed, while frantically tearing off his own clothing. Then, she fell back on the edge of the soft coverlet, and he was suddenly on top of her, touching her neck, her breasts, her thighs, and not being able to wait, he entered her, and all his world seemed a voluptuous dream. He felt more fulfilled than ever before in his lifetime, and wanted never to stop feeling this way!

After a little cry as he came inside her, Mariana, too, felt excited and loved, and found her arms around him, pulling him closer, not wanting him to stop what he was doing. If this was the married state, she liked it and wanted more. For the first time on her wedding day, she felt happy—happier than she had ever been.

Then, their mouths met. She joined her tongue to his, and she wanted him to be inside her now, and stay there forever.

Nine

It was again the beginning of the dry season at Paraiso, just a year after the wedding of Mariana and Carlos.

The outward appearance of the hacienda, in general, was the same, but the mood had much changed.

María Mariana had brought a heart to the place that had been missing the warmth of a real home. Her little son, named for his Uncle Eduardo, had been born almost exactly nine months after the wedding, and had brought with him laughter, gentleness and kindness.

Mariana was a natural mother: sweet, patient and charitable. Everyone around her, from the baby outwards to the servants and field workers benefited from that love.

Carlos, from the first moment, had found passion in his marriage, and had become more outgoing and benevolent in all his endeavors.

However, strangely enough, he loved, but had not fallen in love, with his adoring wife. He treated her with kindness and respect, made love to her often; but something far within his heart remained untouched, in spite of her almost slave-like regard for him. He was her new god.

Fatherhood became him. He doted on Eduardito, and instead of closeting himself in the library, could often be found reading under an arbor, while watching over his tiny son.

The household help seemed to have come alive in the last months, doing their duties with happy faces, so that everything was shiny and polished, from floors to silver, furniture and piano. The curtains were constantly washed and hung over clean windows. And outside, the color of the whole house was again being changed; this time to a soft pink-tinged beige.

Eduardo, too, was happier. He, more than Carlos, had missed their mother's graceful presence, and, having a pretty young sister-in-law gently overseeing the domestic scene touched him in an unforeseen way. He began to yearn for a real role in the household, and a wife of his own. Now twenty-nine, he felt that life was passing him by.

Unlike his brother, Eduardo had little real contact with the actual products of their realm. Carlos came and went, to and fro, from their smaller, surrounding plantations of La Emilia, La Fanny and La Nelly, to the other five, farther-way estates, where cattle, horses, bananas, rubber and coffee were their products, to the enormous cacao groves of the home farm. He, however, did the planning and accounting for all, right in the very house where he had been born; and now ate, slept, studied and worked, almost entirely alone, day after long day and year.

Today, though, he felt less lonely, since old Dr. Mario Cueva was a house guest, and had brought with him his son, Fernando, now also a doctor. Carlos had invited him not only as a friend, but to be sure that Mariana was in good health, since she had been quite pale since giving birth.

Eduardo took the two guests around the grounds, and to visit the nearest cacao grove, dark and shady under the giant palo prieto trees. Pepín and a few other workers accompanied them to demonstrate the steps from harvesting the cacao beans, to drying, storing and packing them for shipping.

Later, when they returned to the cool house, where refreshing drinks were served, Carlos joined them, and the two country gentlemen were treated to all the gossip from town, and, more importantly, the news of the country and from abroad.

The thing that most excited the two doctors, though, was the coming railroad service from Bahía to Chone, which would allow them to travel more comfortably, as well as to receive mail more promptly.

Mariana joined them for dinner, and was complimented for the household, the excellent meal and for her charming presence.

"Senõra Mariana, la felicito. I congratulate you! You have a beautiful son, a lovely home and you, yourself, are the flower of it all!" said the old doctor gallantly.

All nodded and smiled in agreement.

"I can see that living here becomes you!" he added.

Mariana blushed and replied, "Thank you, Doctor, but it is Carlos who does everything—with Eduardo's help, of course!"

Both brothers smilingly denied this.

"So you are happy here in Ecuador, away from your Colombia?"

"Oh, yes, but I do miss my family! Carlos has promised me that they will come soon…maybe to stay, and work here, too…my brothers, that is." And she blushed again. She was used to being in the shadows, looking at her Sun, not being the center of attention.

"Yes, yes," broke in Carlos, as he saw his wife's shyness begin to turn to sadness.

"Eduardo, above all, could use some help, especially now that we are also managing two of our neighbors' lands, to the west and north of us. But still, we must wait a little longer, as we need time to make all the permanent arrangements. We'll need another smaller house to be built next door."

"Yes, indeed!" Eduardo rejoined. "I've been working on the plans with several of our best hands, who are gifted in these matters. We'll need at least four bedrooms and a separate kitchen and dining room. I think it will be like a smaller version of this home, and very convenient for their family."

Mariana, once again in the background, where she was happiest, beamed at the thought of her family moving in permanently…and so close by! She looked at her husband proudly and lovingly. What a good man he was! And how she adored everything about him!

Ten

Dawn was spectacular that June day. Paraiso's bell tolled in the cool air, sending ripples of sound out into the rose and lilac sky. And all who heard began their daily routines.

Mariana stirred at the now-familiar morning call to awake and tried to roll over. She was big again with child, expecting its birth in August. She was back in her own room again, since both she and Carlos felt that they needed to sleep apart these last few months.

Slowly she awoke, and smiled at the sound of her little son, also stirring in his crib next to her bed She opened her eyes and reached for his hand, letting his small fingers curl around hers. She regretted the ongoing change from helpless infant to sturdy toddler, no longer in constant need of her arms.

"Mamá! Buenosdías!" the words slurred together. He sat up, now fully awake. He had learned many phrases and 'talked' all day long.

Mariana was enchanted, and greeted him the same way. Then she added, slowly and clearly,

"¿Cómo amanecistes?" "How are you, on waking?"

He echoed, " 'Com'aman-tes." Slowly she corrected him and he tried the words several times, finally learning them.

There was a knock at the door, it opened and Carlos looked in on them, smiling.

"Buenos días, Papá. ¿Cómo amanecistes?"

Both parents burst out laughing at the little boy's use of the 'familiar' address to his father.

"I? I'm fine! Thank you."

Carlos was in a good mood, happy that at last his wife would now have company besides his own.

For her family was due to arrive very soon, perhaps even today! They were coming by carriage, then on the railroad from Guayaquil, changing at Bahía for Chone.

They had exchanged many letters, and Carlos was quite sure that they must now be very near.

The pleasant, smaller house next door was now finished and waiting. It was completely furnished, right down to the pots and pans in the kitchen. One of the housemaids, Licha, would now work over there; and Dela's daughter, Zenaida (or 'Zeni') would be their cook.

"Come, mi amor, get up and dress! And I'll send nurse Rosa to change Eduardito. Apúre, hurry, this may be the day!"

He strode over to his wife, bent and kissed her, then the baby, and left the room with a wave.

Downstairs, there was excitement in the air, and a general bustle of activity. This might be the day the family would be bigger, and the servants could hardly contain their happiness.

Like births, deaths, shipments on their way, or some accident or illness, company, now to be permanent, to an isolated place was the very pinnacle of news and wonder!

For Eduardo, too, the fact that Mariana's family was arriving was exciting. He liked them all, and looked forward to working with Felipe and Alfonso. He had a premonition that they would be good friends.

"Ñaño, 'brother'," he asked Carlos. "Have you already sent Pepín to Chone? I think it's a good idea to be waiting, as they suggested, at the 'Hotel Majestad'."

"Yes," answered Carlos, "He left at the bell's ringing this morning."

As they started breakfast, Mariana joined them, and Rosa carried little Eduardo to the kitchen, to feed him there.

"Carlos, I believe I'll go and inspect the casita this morning, just to make sure there are enough linens and kitchen supplies. Will Pepín bring back some flour and lard?"

"Yes, my dear, he will. And yes, give the little house a final inspection. It's a good idea...by the way, what do you want to name the place?"

Mariana thought a moment, and answered,

"I've been thinking about that. Maybe we could call it 'La Colombiana', for my grandfather?"

"Yes, yes, good idea," rejoined her husband.

And Eduardo, too, seemed to like the name.

So the morning passed busily, until, at last, seeing some dust down the road, they all gathered at the main entrance, hoping it was the party from Chone.

And, sure enough, there was Pepín on horseback, leading a carriage down the main road, approaching the house at a fast clip. Several faces peered from the small windows, with arms waving on both sides.

The moment they came to a halt, down jumped Mara, followed by her brothers and grandfather.

She ran to Mariana and threw her arms around her sister.

"Oh, I'm so glad to see you at last! It's been so long!"

The María Margarita who spoke had grown taller and slimmer at eleven years, with long legs and arms that had tanned on her long journey from Colombia.

Her hair was still blonde, but now a burnished yellow, streaked with darker gold. Her bright summer-sky eyes danced with the same mischievous glints as she took in the family of Paraiso.

"Oh, it's good to be here! Thank you for inviting us!"

All the travelers were dusting themselves off as they joined Mara to shake hands all around.

The General was now more than eighty years old, and the last few difficult years in Colombia were etched on his face.

As soon as they noticed this, both Carlos and Eduardo hastened to bring the weary old man inside so he could be seated in a comfortable chair, and all could be served cold drinks.

Pepín, meanwhile, had his helpers transfer the large pile of luggage, cases and boxes to the new, smaller house where Licha and Zenaida received them, being sure that the workers and their dusty sandals did not step more than three feet into the polished interior.

In the large sala, or main living room of the larger home, the tired new arrivals were beginning to revive a little from their long journey. The two younger men, Felipe and Alfonso, now twenty-five and nineteen, were in earnest conversation with the two older planters, and soon-to-be role models.

The General had dozed off in his cane rocking chair. Mara and Mariana were all smiles, with frequent hugs and kisses joining them, as they perched on a large couch of woven toquillo in a corner of the semi-darkened room, cooling themselves with ornate fans.

Carlos was the first to break away and suggest that the company would probably enjoy a bath and change of clothes; and perhaps, a siesta before dinner in the big house.

This suited everyone, and they all rose and went to see their new home for the first time.

Eleven

The 'new' family quickly adjusted to their unaccustomed country life: exploring the perimeter of the cleared land, venturing into the deeply shaded, rather mysterious cacao groves, and becoming familiar with the daily routines of the people who lived and worked in this hidden world.

Mara, especially, grew to love the places she had first known at an even younger age. She could be seen in the animal barns, the vegetable fields or down near the Garrapata River that flowed below the gardens. She wore large straw hats and high boots for protection, but still bronzed under the unrelenting sun.

Some days, though, she spent indoors, reading her lessons to her sister, or playing with little Eduardito.

The new baby was expected any time now, and Mariana spent most days on a lounge chair in the cool 'sala', where darker curtains had been hung over the gauze ones, to relieve the glare.

She did not feel her usual bright self, and hardly spoke unless to answer direct questions. Carlos was worried about her tired passivity, and had once again summoned Dr. Cueva. But the old gentleman had sent his regrets, and his son, Fernando, arrived in his stead.

After an examination, he began giving Mariana three daily glasses of a potent, natural vitamin remedy, whose bitter taste belied its great value.

With his care, Mariana began to feel better and could again laugh and play with her son.

Little Jaime was born soon after, in August. And, by the time the rains arrived in late November, he was a strong little baby.

Mariana, though giving him her milk, was not feeling as well as after her first son's birth. Dr. Fernando had stayed on to oversee her care, and pronounced her anemic, as she had lost a great deal of blood during the birth.

Now, she hardly left the house. Two young servants became nursemaids, and between them, kept the little boy and tiny baby bathed, dressed and fed.

Mara, watching over her sister, grew worried and lonesome. Carlos, who had long ago thought of bringing young Pilar Gallardo to Paraiso, now acted on his impulse and rode over to discuss the idea with his neighbor, Rafael.

"Both girls are quite ignorant," he said frankly to Pilar's parents, "and both are quite alone. If you'll allow her, Pilar could stay with María Margarita in the 'new' house, and both could learn their lessons together, with Don Francisco. Father Juan has also offered to teach them. Between these two, I think they will become quite educated young ladies! What do you think, Don Rafael?!"

"Yes, I suppose you're right, but Doña Otavia and I would sorely miss our girl!"

"But you're free to visit her anytime! In fact, I insist upon it! Come, first, and see if you approve of the living quarters. And, we *are* right next door you know, not in another country!"

Both men laughed, but Maria Otavia looked worried, and turned to her only child with a protective glance. She did not approve of the proposed plans, but felt helpless, as usual, against the weight of men's decisions.

"Rafa," she pleaded, "she is too young! And she is quite happy here with us!"

"I know, my dear one, but we must give her a chance, too, to know more than this small farm."

In the end, a compromise was reached. After all, Rafael now owed thousands of sucres to Carlos, who had been financing his operations for the last few years. True, their cacao production was far higher than before, but he now had almost no control over it.

And he knew, too, that Carlos was right. He was raising a very pretty but totally uneducated girl, who knew only cookery and needlework. Besides, he had himself envisioned sending her to school in Chone, with the nuns, and later introducing her to the finer families there where she might find a solid husband.

Now, the men agreed that the families should share their next Sunday comida at Paraiso, and see if the girls were still as compatible as before. If so, Pilar would try living there for a week or two before making permanent arrangements.

And so, on a wet and humid afternoon, in early December, Pilar arrived with her parents, and several bundles of belongings.

Nothing on this dreary day could have brightened life more for Mara!

Twelve

The rainy season was stormy and steamy that winter, but the two girls at Paraiso were as happy together as only best friends can be. At first, Pilar missed being the center of her parents' loving attention, but grew content with their frequent visits.

Neither girl had ever learned more than rudimentary reading, but now were plunged into intensive study.

Francisco Villalobos, though a somewhat vain and pedantic man, was, for all that, an excellent maestro. He was now approaching sixty, and had grown quite bent with years of study behind him. His hair was scant and stringy, but he compensated for that with bushy black mustachios that drooped down on either side of his thin red lips.

He was meticulously punctual, and arrived daily at the main house shortly after the tolling of the six a.m. bell. There, he breakfasted alone at one end of the long dinning room before entering the library, now also the school room.

Daily, the two twelve-year-olds had their first meal in the 'new' house next door, then arrived shortly after to study until the 'comida' at one p.m. Then they were expected to do at least one and a half hours of unsupervised homework in the afternoon.

At this pace, they had already covered many chapters of 'Don Quixote', knew basic arithmetic, and were beginning the study of the geography of the Americas.

This morning, they had been promised free reading time should they be able to name all the rivers and bays of Manabí. Between the two they accomplished this, so Maestro Francisco kept his word and left them alone for half an hour, while he paced up and down in the garden.

Mischievous as they were, Mara and Pilar knew better than to play in the sacrosanct library. Besides, they had long been curious about the 'grown up' books.

So the two made their choices and settled into the deep, woven armchairs to read and dream. Neither one understood much of what she read, but the gold-edged books were illustrated handsomely, and that helped them, even with their limited vocabulary.

Back promptly in half an hour, Sr. Francisco began a new lesson in the dreaded subject: arithmetic! During this time, they were interrupted by the appearance of Eduardo, who, after taking in the scene, apologized, picked up a book from the table, and left them again. It was hard for the two older brothers to break the habits of many years.

While the rest of the household grew accustomed to the new routines, Mariana was left more and more alone. She had never quite returned to her former active self, and the whole family was shocked when it became known that she was pregnant again.

By this time, Carlos had convinced the young Dr. Cueva to relinquish his private practice in Chone in order to stay on permanently at El Paraiso. This was not difficult, since life here was tranquil and the young doctor had a real affection for all the family, especially Mariana.

As the months went by, her appearance changed dramatically. In spite of carrying a child, she became thinner, and her large green eyes had a haunted look.

Carlos, too, suffered with her. He began to wake during the nights, pace the hallways, check on the babies, then pace again, until he, too, lost weight and became withdrawn and quick-tempered.

It seemed that all the hacienda operated in a hush. The news that the sweet Señora was ill affected all, from the kitchen to the fields. Father Juan performed the Mass outdoors, so that all the faithful could attend, and offered up special prayers for his benefactress.

So the winter months passed, and the dry season began once more. But the cooler weather seemed to bring no relief to the troubles at El Paraiso.

Thirteen

Dr. Fernando had been given a permanent room in the main house so as to be near Mariana. She was very close to the time of delivery, and was never left alone.

Even Mara spent at least an hour at her bedside every day. She was a natural little nurse, and the doctor found her so useful that Carlos gave her permission to stop her schoolwork altogether, while Mariana needed her.

Sometimes she read to her sister; at others, Mariana would shake her head, close her eyes, and Mara would just hold her hand, saying nothing.

Her husband was frantic, used as he was to righting everything on Paraiso. Here, he was helpless. He tried to supervise the little boys' routines, to keep the household running normally, but he was unable to issue any meaningful orders.

So it fell to Eduardo to oversee the inside and outside help, making it possible for his brother to be with his little family all day. And the plantation continued in its usual cycles.

Pepín had become more and more reliable, acting as a lieutenant to Ernesto Cucalón, the titular overseer. Here there were subtle undertones in the relationship. Cucalón was a mestizo, part Spanish, part native Ecuadorian, of Indian descent, with an accompanying inferiority complex. Pepín was pure Indian, but proud of his heritage; working for the all-white criollo dueños, or owners, and taking orders from a half-breed.

Eduardo had always trusted Pepín, a man with no complexes, open and above-board in all his relationships. Cucalón saw this rapport and was secretly jealous and resentful. He did not intend to be merely an overseer all his life.

These daily undercurrents bothered Eduardo, who was relieved that Carlos did not need to worry about them at the moment; for he was blunt and tactless at times, while his younger brother was patient and careful not to offend.

This late May morning, Eduardo had worked since rising with the bell, and, a few hours later, closed his record books and went into the main house. He was silently appreciating the Palacios Uribe men, Felipe and Alfonso. Ever since their arrival last year, it had been easier to run the hacienda. They were young, energetic and intelligent, and were quickly learning all facets of the cacao trade. In fact, a new shipment was ready to leave this very day, bound for Bahía de Caráquez and abroad.

Felipe and Alfonso were down at the river at this moment, overseeing the loading of the barges. True, the river level was very low now compared to the winter torrent, but the waterway experts agreed that there was sufficient depth and current to safely float them to the larger Chone River below, before continuing on to the coast.

By force of old habit, Eduardo found himself standing at the library door, but he remembered the changes and knocked before entering.

There, Pilar sat alone with Father Juan Bautista, who was giving her a catechism lesson.

"I'm sorry to interrupt," said Eduardo, as the flustered priest rose, and motioned Pilar to do the same.

"No, please, sit down! Continue! I just came to get my book." He picked up a large volume, trying not to stare.

But he had just seen Pilar for the first time—really noticed her as a person!

Her dark hair fell almost to her waist, partially covering her carved-ivory features. She looked at him through long dark lashes, her eyes a subtle hazel.

His heart lurched, and in that instant he was lost! He could not believe what his feelings were saying to him! Impossible that a man of thirty-two years could look at a young girl of twelve and be drowned in this powerful ocean of hitherto unknown emotions that flooded his being. For a moment, he could not breathe, his face became heated and flushed, and he turned and stumbled out of the room.

All down the hallway, he chastised himself. Was he a monster, some kind of abnormal animal that he should be so attracted to a *girl*?! He vowed to stay away from her, and partly walked, partly stumbled back to his private office sanctuary, hoping to lose himself in his work…

This was to be a memorable day for all at El Paraiso. Mariana had felt some contractions and had called out weakly. Mara ran to get Carlos and the doctor. Both came running to the sick room; the doctor to attend his patient, the husband to protest that it was far too early for the baby to arrive.

"Mariana, my love, try *not* to push!" begged Carlos.

Dr. Fernando urged him to move aside so that he could listen to his two patients' hearts: the mother's and the child's. The former's was not encouraging and he could barely hear the baby's.

"Don Carlos, there is really nothing you can do here. I beg you to leave us alone. Marita and Doña Mercedes, 'Dulce', can be of assistance in case of emergency. Meanwhile, we'll just keep the Señora quiet and try to stop the contractions."

But, no sooner had he said this, than Mariana cried out, and a large amount of blood soaked through the white sheets.

"Ay, doctor, me duele mucho…I'm in great pain! Please make it stop!" She half-sat up as another contraction seemed to tear her apart.

"Señora, Doña Mariana," pleaded the doctor, with tears in his eyes at her pain. "Please lie back down. I am going to give you something to help." And he took a large spoon from the nurse and filled it with a dark liquid.

No sooner had Mariana drunk the medicine than she lay back on her pillows, and was limp and quiet. For a long half-hour, all was peaceful in the room, while Mara and nurse Dulce attempted to replace the soiled sheets with clean white ones.

Carlos, who had been at the door when his wife cried out, returned to her bedside, and refused to move.

"Why was God punishing him?" he wondered bitterly. "What have I done?! She is too young, too needed here!"

But in his heart he heard the answer: "You have not loved her enough, as she deserved. Your eyes and your thoughts were ever wandering, when *she* should have been your everything!"

"Carlos..." He barely heard his name whispered by an awakening Mariana.

"Thank you...for being my husband...for being such a good father."

He could barely hear her soft voice, and leaned down to her face, tears welling in his eyes: tears of love and compassion, and tears of guilt and remorse.

Suddenly, in the extreme quiet of the room, all noticed a new stain of red spreading over the sheets.

"Oh!" cried Mariana, as the baby was expelled into the doctor's waiting hands.

But, instead of the familiar joyous cry of birth, the room seemed enveloped in the absolute silence that followed. Only a soft sigh came from the mother, and all standing around her knew in their hearts that they would never hear a sound from her again.

Fourteen

As her living there had affected them, now Mariana's death pervaded the lives of those who lived and worked on El Paraiso. A general malaise fell over the plantation as palpable as a fog covering the swampy shores of the Garrapata on a winter morning.

The spirit of cooperation that had existed among the workers, now seemed to have turned to bitterness-like the taste of cacao seeds spat out by marauding birds. Clashes became common among the men, and squabbles arose readily in the women's quarters.

In the main house, too, a permanent shadow seemed to hover over the inhabitants. Daily life continued automatically, with no interest or joy.

Mara, especially, felt abandoned, with no one to guide her or lift her spirits. She attended her classes again, but her studies suffered and the bright light of her eyes seemed to be extinguished forever.

Pilar tried with all her girlish might to help her, but a wall had grown up between the two. At last, Pilar, not understanding the depth of Mara's loss, also began to feel abandoned and begged Carlos to let her return home to 'San Rafael'. He, listless and incapable of reaching out from his interior grief, just nodded permission. So, when her parents next came for their bi-monthly visit, a tearful Pilar returned home with them.

Only Mariana's two brothers seemed to be able to rise above their loss and take a lead in the management of the hacienda. For reasons unknown to them, their role-model, Eduardo, seemed as lost as his older brother, Carlos. As a result, when it came time for the bi annual meeting with the bankers in Portoviejo, Eduardo declined the honor, sending, instead, his two ablest assistants.

Portoviejo, the capital of Manabí province, was, in 1912, a bustling city, on the banks of the Portoviejo River, 40 miles inland from the pacific coast; and it made Chone appear merely a large village. It boasted many schools, parks and churches as well as a modern hospital, just being built.

The young ambassadors felt exhilarated and privileged to represent the Castañeda brothers, whose agricultural acumen was so widely known and admired; and who were unique in that they were personally present to manage their lands, unlike the majority of the owners of extensive properties elsewhere: 'haciendados' who were mostly absentee proprietors, living in large cities, or even abroad.

The bankers made them feel welcome, and the handsome young Colombians made a favorable and memorable impression on the businessmen.

"As you know," they told the two, "our bank is representing several regional groups here in Manabí, and we hope it will not be long before a national entity can be established."

"Meantime," continued a prosperous looking gentleman in his mid-fifties, "We will strive to continue our combined loans to the leaders of this province. In your case, however, the gains of the last six months at El Paraiso have greatly exceeded the loan made! So you two men can return with more than a clean slate! Here are some documents you can take back," he said, handing them a small pile of papers.

"Beyond this personal information, we will have two days of meetings and discussions concerning our expansion in this area. I sincerely hope you can attend!"

He stopped to light a cigar, and smiled over the flame of the match. "And please be so kind as to attend a dinner my wife and I are hosting this evening."

At their nods and expressions of assent, he rapidly penned an address and handed the paper to Felipe.

"We'll see you at eight o'clock, then," he smiled.

As soon as the meeting for the day ended, the brothers left. It was still early and they decided to walk around this area of the city before returning to freshen themselves at their hotel.

Not to get lost, or be late, they took a horse-drawn cab to the address given them, and arrived punctually at eight o'clock.

The banker's residence was large but not intimidating; simply constructed of wood. At the plain entrance door, a maid-servant dressed in black, with a white apron and headband, answered their ring. She showed them into a hallway, where they left their hats and white gloves.

They could hear soft conversation and laughter from the room beyond, and entered it to see a dozen or so elegantly gowned women and well-dressed men.

"Good evening," they said in unison, and the hostess came forward to welcome them.

"Please come in;" and they were introduced all around.

Felipe was immediately struck by the appearance of a young woman called 'Elena', whose dark hair was pulled back into a bun revealing strong, striking features on a pale face above a long, graceful neck, her throat covered with three strands of pearls. Luckily, he was seated next to her at dinner, while poor Alfonso had to settle for a middle-aged married lady, with suspiciously blond hair.

Thus, their first venture into the world of finance began! By the time they returned to El Paraiso, their destinies would have a new direction.

Fifteen

On their return to El Paraiso, the two Palacios men seemed invigorated and ready to work and learn more than ever.

There began a lively exchange of letters between Felipe and Elena Mendoza, for the attraction had been mutual.

Almost twenty-six, Felipe was ready for matrimony, but his younger brother was eager to explore all the many possibilities that life suddenly seemed to offer him.

Eduardo was pleasantly surprised to see such positive energy in his protégés, and was still grateful for having, himself, avoided the 'outside' trip. He was happily miserable at the thoughts he had of Pilar, who was on his mind and heart from daybreak to dark, and then in his dreams.

He had not seen her since her departure over a month ago. He thought up reasons why he should ride over to 'San Rafael', but Carlos acted on *his* impulses first.

The older brother had gone there several times during the last month, ostensibly to discuss crops with Don Rafael. But, unbeknownst to Eduardo, Carlos, too, was more and more conscious of Pilar as a ripening beauty. Her parents, though, especially Doña Otavia, were not blind to the probable cause for these visits, and, lately, the mother had sequestered their daughter whenever a rider was seen cantering in their direction.

This forced Carlos's hand, and he mentioned how lonely Mara was, and that she yearned for her friend and classmate.

In the end, the confused parents allowed their daughter to return to 'El Paraiso'.

Now, almost thirteen, like Mara, Pilar packed her few possessions and looked forward to seeing her best friend once again.

Alfonso, now open to meeting females, was instantly taken with the newly-returned girl. But he saw her primarily as a sister and Mara's companion. He was more inclined to accept the invitations sent to him from other plantations, where he knew eligible young women lived.

Eduardo was so afraid of accidentally meeting Pilar that he closeted himself in his office from early morning to night; often having a meal served there on a tray instead of mixing with the family in the dinning room.

Carlos prowled the house's hallways, totally annoyed with himself, but unable to stop his imagination. Mariana's death had been a blow to his psyche. He had not realized how much he had valued her adoration, and missed being the center of her life.

He had been faithful, in fact, for their few, short married years, but now could scarcely control himself. He knew he could not, and should not, have Pilar, yet he bristled when any other male was near her.

Finally, seeing his brother did not want to leave his office duties, he volunteered to go into Chone, himself, to get some much needed supplies. Once there, he reverted to his old ways, and spent almost a week ridding himself of his frustrations.

On the ride home, accompanied by a driver and a wagon full of store goods, his thoughts were gloomy. In four days, he had lost all that he had gained, physically and spiritually, from his four years with Mariana. His conscience black, he vowed to forget thoughts of women, young or not, and live the life of a monk, for as long as he could endure it!

It was years since he had been to confession, but now he sought out the 'new' priest, Father Benedicto Romero, an intellectual Jesuit, brought there to join Father Juan Bautista in ministering to all the farms' populations.

Now, though, a frowning Carlos waited in the tiny chapel's confessional, anxious and fearful of his own long list of misdeeds, dark thoughts and aberrations.

The priest questioned him and he answered in a low and serious tone, naming all the devilish acts, especially in his recent life.

As a penance, the priest ordered him to say ten Hail Marys, dwelling on each of his sins as he did so. He should also pray the rosary each evening, in the chapel. And eat alone for ten days, so as not to be distracted by straying, sinful thoughts. He then blessed him and gave him absolution.

Carlos, meek for the first time in his thirty-seven years, obeyed, and vowed to the priest, and to himself, to cleanse this heart and mind.

Sixteen

"Pilar! It's so wonderful to have you here again!" Mara was excited, as she finished combing her long hair. For a moment, she held it up off her neck to see how she would look next year, when she could officially be a 'young lady'.

"Oh, it's so pretty that way! I'd love to have your golden hair!"

"How can you say that!? You have the bluest-black hair, like a real thoroughbred! It's so lovely!"

Pilar blushed, as she wasn't used to receiving compliments; if looking like a horse was one! This brought a small smile to her pink lips.

The two held hands as they descended the staircase, on the way to their lessons in the library. No one else was about. Each girl had breakfasted; one in the smaller house next door, and one here, in the large dinning room, accompanied only by her two brothers.

The home seemed strangely empty. The servants were all in the kitchen at this time of the morning, and the two proprietors were hardly ever seen nowadays.

This gave the house an air of a holiday, as even their teacher was to be absent today. He had given them a list of work to do, starting with mathematics and ending with Latin and literature. They were excused for the day after one o'clock, a real vacation!

Both girls, obedient by nature and training, dutifully did their algebra, quietly and independently. Then, they practiced reading their Latin aloud to each other, answering the questions at the end of the lesson.

After this, they were free to read their books for the last hour of their study period.

Mara settled herself in her comfortable chair to read from her current favorite, 'War and Peace'. As she sat there in the sunlight that reflected off her golden head, she realized subconsciously that her best friend somewhat resembled Tolstoy's heroine, Natasha, but was prettier, more like his brunette Sonia.

But the heroine was, apart from her coloring, much like the reader, a free and happy spirit! Mara was totally transported to Russia!

Pilar, though, favored poetry, and had read through several collections since their studies had begun. Today, she selected an unknown volume, much used, with slightly tattered pages.

She read the first few poems, then leafed through the heavy book to find others more to her liking. As she raised the thick tome, a scrap of paper fell to the floor, and she stooped to pick it up.

Frowning, she read the faded ink writing, a poem of passion. For the second time, she tried to understand the words, clearly written in a hurry and under stress.

"Mara," she called from her corner of the room. "Mara!"

Her companion was so deep into her story, now of a Russia at war, with the hero lying amid bodies strewn across a sunlit field, that she was slow to return to the reality of a hacienda in Ecuador!

She blinked, then focused on Pilar, who was showing her a rumpled piece of paper with barely legible scribbles in ink strewn across it.

"What is this?! "

"A poem, I think, that fell out of my book. Can you decipher it?"

"Well," said Mara, squinting, "let me see." Suddenly she looked up at Pilar, and a mischievous smile crossed her face.

"This says 'Pilar'!!"

"What?!" Pilar's pale face began to redden.

"Yes, listen…" read Mara.

" 'Mi amor secreto
Encerrado en mi pecho-
Con cara de Madona,
O, Pilar, mi adorada!'…and so on!…
("My secret love
Enclosed in my breast-

With the face of a Madonna,
Oh, Pilar, my adored one!)
"It's not a very good poem!!"
Pilar bowed her head, completely mortified.
"Who could have said these things!?"
"Well, *not* Maestro Francisco, for sure!" answered Mara, laughing.
"Who is left?!" Pilar asked in a muffled voice.
"Only Don Carlos or Don Eduardo. I'm sure it's not Father Benedicto!" Mara giggled.
When she saw that Pilar was not amused, but chagrined, Mara tried to cheer her up, saying,
"It's one o'clock! Let's go cool off in the river!"
"But we've been told not to go down there alone!" worried Pilar.
"We'll be together! Besides, that was because the field workers were down there cutting manglar roots for a month, and they're gone now. We'll be safe!"
So the two decided to skip the midday meal and go down to the Garrapata River for a refreshing swim.
The water there was only waist-deep in the middle of the rock-strewn stream, not much more than a deep creek, here at the foot of the garden. The many giant trees, mangroves and palo prietos, hid them from the house.
At first, they were demure, just wading, lifting their long skirts. But, not satisfied with wetting only their feet, they decided to remove all their clothes, to dip, neck deep, into the cool water.
Now it was evident that the two had passed from childhood. Both girls had soft curves and uplifted breasts that were already full and well developed. Together, they were unselfconscious, yet they were vigilant, afraid their prank would be discovered; especially since their clothing lay on the rocks, now out of reach.
"¡Muchachas! ¿Enqué están pensando?!
¿Qué hacen aquí?!" ("Girls! What are you thinking of?! What are you doing here?!"), They heard a familiar voice scolding.
Dulce stood watching them, arms akimbo, attempting to look stern.

As they rushed, dripping, from the stream, their nurse and ally quickly covered their naked bodies.

"Luckily I saw you headed this way," said the ever-vigilant servant.

"What if it had been your brothers, or, worse yet, the señores dueños?! Oh, the shame!"

Yet she spoke mildly, and with a flickering smile across her wrinkled face.

She remembered, all too well, the joys of girlhood, and the delight of disobedience.

Seventeen

It had been more than two years, now, since Mariana had died. Many were the times when Eduardo yearned to speak to Pilar, who was fast becoming a woman. But in all this time he had carefully avoided her.

A few weeks ago, he had taken an early morning stroll, to stretch, after sitting in his office since daybreak.

The dew was still on the damp ground, strewn with palm fronds from a strong wind the evening before. At this hour, many birds decorated the branches and flew to and fro, calling out to one another. A wild parrot and his mate made a streak of color, red and green, as they flew from the garden to their home in the jungle.

As Eduardo changed direction to return to the house, head down, lost in thought, his foot stepped on something white, and he heard a gasp.

There, face to face with him, was the object of the torment of his mind and heart. It took his breath away, and he could only stare at Pilar, who, also speechless, pointed to his foot.

His boot was covering a lacy handkerchief, and, after an initial paralysis, he recovered, bent down and extracted the now-muddy object.

"I'm so sorry-perdóneme, excuse me, please!" Eduardo, not wishing to put a soiled object into the hands of this lovely creature, held the handkerchief for a moment, then tucked it into his vest pocket.

"I'll deliver this to the laundress, Señorita Pilar. Again, forgive me!"

Pilar, hearing herself called 'Señorita' by a gentleman she had admired and respected since childhood, was confused, but inwardly pleased. She smiled, said, "It's all right. Thank you," and started to move away.

"Pilar!!" Eduardo could not let her go.

"Pilar," he repeated, loving the sound on his tongue. "Please stay a moment. I've been meaning to speak to you!"

Now Pilar, no longer amused, was thoroughly confused.

"All right. Here I am."

"Pilar," started Eduardo again. Suddenly he grasped her hands in his, no longer able to contain the love he had felt for so long.

"Please let me tell you how much you mean to me"! I want us to be friends, more than friends, forever! Do you understand me? I love you, Pilar!"

The dam had burst, and Eduardo felt both an enormous relief and a superhuman strength. He clasped the girl in his strong arms, and gently kissed the top of her head.

She, taken totally by surprise, looked up at this gentle man who had been her brother, father, teacher, and saw the truth in his eyes. She was moved, as never before in her young life, by some power beyond her control, and, as his lips came down on hers, she succumbed to them, welcomed them, and returned his ardor.

Then, his arms pulled her to his chest, and hers answered by reaching up around his neck, acknowledging his passion, welcoming it.

"Oh, Pilar!" gasped the lover, "I have to tell you! I never want to let you go! Please, please be my wife!"

And they kissed again, this time deep into each other.

"Answer me, my adored one. Tell me you will!"

Pilar broke away a little, her heart racing, her head spinning with this sudden avalanche engulfing her. But she knew, not as a girl, but as a woman, that this man was good for her, and that she had just been honored beyond all imagination!

"Yes," she said softly. "I *want* to be your wife!" And she felt his hand cup her face, and lift it up for a shower of kisses: on her forehead, her eyelids, her cheeks, until their mouths met again in a passionate encounter.

Together, they half-walked, half-stumbled back to the house, where, flushed and smiling, they had their first breakfast together.

Eighteen

"Ñañito, little brother, come, let's walk together to the grove. I need to check on the pods, but I also need to talk with you!"

Carlos beckoned to Eduardo, who, surprised, rose from his desk, put on his helmet and joined his brother. He was feeling nervous, also wanting to confide in him. He hadn't yet said anything about his engagement to Pilar, and had been loathe to spoil their secret.

They began to walk the short distance to the drying racks, where Carlos stopped a moment to feel the pulp, turning one handful over. One of the workers came running to inquire if they should turn all the sacs, but Carlos just said briefly,

"No, they're all right. Wait until nightfall, then cover them."

The worker nodded and turned away with, "Sí, Don Carlos. I'll give the order."

The two men continued on to the nearest cacao grove, and went from bright sunlight into dimness, under the high canopy of protective palo prieto trees.

"Hermano," began Carlos, I need you to know. I'm going to marry again."

Eduardo stopped, his heart pounding, not wanting to hear.

"Yes? Really? So soon?" was all he could get out.

Carlos regarded him curiously. This was not the reaction he'd expected from his always-dependable younger brother. "'So soon?'" he repeated. "Two years is not really 'soon'! I loved Mariana," he said, more like a litany than a vow from the heart.

"But I have two fast-growing sons," he continued. "they need a mother, and I need a woman."

"Yes, but…who?" asked Eduardo, inwardly flinching, not wanting to hear the answer.

"Well," replied Carlos, sitting down on a stump, motioning his brother to join him.

"I've thought about this for a long time. I've rejected any town woman…it's got to be someone used to the country, and our way of life…"

And then he said the dreaded name!

"Pilar might do…*could* do…but her family is not up to ours. Doña Otavia is already montubia, and I don't want mestizo mixing with the criollo line…"

Eduardo was first amazed, and then angry, reddening as he heard this almost flippant mention of his life's most precious gift!

"Stop!" he said raspingly. "you've said enough! Pilar and I are engaged to be married! She is the best thing ever to come into my life!"

Carlos jumped up, protesting, himself incredulous.

"Eduardo! Brother! Please…I meant no disparagement…forgive me, but I feel stunned at this news! When did this happen?!"

Eduardo calmed down immediately, again his usual tranquil self, and said in a low voice,

"The truth is, I've been in love with her for two years, but tried to stay away from her…she being so very young!

But, a few weeks ago, we met by accident, and…it seems…I am so lucky…she loves me, too!"

Carlos, amazed, mumbled,

"Well…my…congratulations…I confess I'm very surprised…and pleased, of course!"

"Thank you," Eduardo said, formally; and not wanting to discuss his now-spoiled secret further, went on,

"Please, tell me about *your* plans!"

"Oh, yes…well, though I've said nothing yet, I plan to speak to Mara."

"Mara!" It was Eduardo's turn to be amazed.

"But she, too, is so young…and you, brother, are even older than I!"

"I know, there are twenty-five years between us. But, think of it! It's logical…she's Mariana's sister…sweet, and very bright! She'll be wonderful with your 'tocayo'…namesake…and Jaimito. And, I must admit, she grows more appealing to me every day!"

"Appealing, yes," replied Eduardo. "But surely you'd want a mutual love! She's such a free spirit…she'll be hard to tame!"

"I've no doubt we'll grow to love each other, but, as you've pointed out, I'm not getting any younger, and I don't want to wait too long! Maybe we can have a double wedding!"

Eduardo felt torn between two loyalties: not wanting to surrender his private life, but not wanting to disappoint his closest friend and relative.

At this moment, Pepín came into the grove, speaking to his fellow-laborer, Oswaldo. When he saw the two señores/dueños, he stopped speaking and looked guilty. His friend had been giving him news of his cousin in Guayaquil, where the plantation workers were being 'given' their own plots of land to sow and harvest. While Oswaldo didn't know all the details yet, he was excited and said that Señor Cucalón was advising all the men to demand this, too.

What they hadn't been told, was that half of what they grew would go back to the owners, and, more importantly, that they would give up a salary in exchange for four days' labor on the hacendado's (or landowner's) property.

This plan, already used widely, especially in the Andean highlands, was known as 'huasipungo'; the workers were 'huasipungueros'. This practice reduced these Indians to virtual slavery-demeaning them, and subjecting whole populations to a life of unending poverty.

The Castañedas had never liked relinquishing land to anyone, and had always preferred to pay their workers and provide free housing, and a convenient non-profit store of provisions.

Luckily for the men, and the overseer Cucalón, the two brothers overhead nothing, and simply greeted the men, and passed out into the sunlit compound of their home.

Nineteen

"Mara, may I speak with you?"

Carlos was half-way through the library door.

Mara looked up from her lesson, and asked Father Benedito if that would be all right.

"Yes, yes, my dear: it's all right…go ahead."

So Mara rose, with a puzzled frown, and joined Carlos in the hallway.

"Come, let's go to the morning room."

This was the pleasant alcove near the much larger dining room. It had a small table and several large woven straw chairs from Jipijapa. Their comfortable pillows had a large floral pattern, and the walls, the only papered ones in the house, were covered with a green fern motif.

Mara, more puzzled than ever, followed her brother-in-law and sat on the edge of a chair, as if preparing to bolt, if necessary.

Carlos, apparently completely calm, was, in reality, not quite sure how to broach the subject that had been on his mind for weeks.

"Mara," he began. "I know it's been lonely for you, except for Pilar's presence, of course, since Mariana left us…

He paused, and Mara, looking down, nodded.

"Well," continued Carlos, "it's been very hard on our two little boys, too. Luckily for them, you've entertained them daily, but, well, it's not the same as having a mother."

Mara, sensing a change of subject, looked up, her blue eyes questioning.

Carlos felt that piercing glance, and almost lost his habitual poise.

"Hmm," he cleared his throat. "Yes…well…not only the boys, but

I, too, have been very lonely…very alone…and now I feel I must remedy this situation." He stopped, smoothing his mustache.

Mara, suddenly having an inkling of where this conversation was leading, felt her clasped hands become damp.

And Carlos went on, "There is only one person in the world, Mara, that could possibly take the place of Mariana. And that person is *you*! Mara, do you think you could find it in your heart to become my wife?"

To say that the young girl was amazed at this proposal would not express the torrent of emotions that rushed over her at that instant! She was speechless!

This man, this brother, this father-figure in her life! What could a girl of fourteen think of this idea!? Become the wife of Mariana's husband!?

All her young life, her reading had led her to believe that true love is the destiny of all…and that *her* love was waiting for her somewhere, as soon as she received some kind of mysterious message. It had only to be deciphered!

Was this, then, that message?! Right here, in the same place she had returned to more than three years ago?! Was this to be her future?!

Thoroughly confused, she was unable to answer, and blushed deeply.

Carlos, realizing her dilemma, was instantly paternal.

"Now, now, Marita, don't be upset. You just have to get used to the idea, and I know that takes time…and," he added slyly, "don't you think we could enjoy ourselves together?"

"Enjoy?" repeated Mara dully.

"Yes, we can do things together. I can teach you many things, and I know I can learn from you, too!"

She simply could not get the idea into her head, and looked, perplexed, at her feet.

"Come, Marita linda," coaxed Carlos, now not quite so paternal. "Let's start getting to know each other better." And he leaned down to kiss her pouty lips.

When she didn't respond, he pulled her up, close to him, holding her in a tight embrace.

"That's better," and he kissed her again, this time more searchingly, opening her mouth.

Mara, feeling nothing, but unable to resist this man she was so used to obeying, let him continue his embrace, his hands now moving to cup her breasts.

"Marita, Marita! You darling girl!"

She felt ready to faint, her head spinning.

"Please," she gasped, "Please let me go!"

Frustrated, and now angered, Carlos released her.

"Very well! Let's not make any decisions today. But get the idea into your head, María Margarita! You're going to be my wife!"

And he let her stumble out of the room, and on over to the house next door.

He stood there in the small room, a big man, feeling defeated by a mere girl!

Twenty

Carlos was doubly frustrated at life these days. First, Mara managed to escape his presence from morning until night. This was made easier for her because the cacao production was it its height and everyone who could work was engaged in helping in the groves, or in readying the crop for shipment.

Even Eduardo was called into action, and had to desert his office for most of the daylight hours, with only Alfonso to help him.

Felipe had gone on another banking errand to Portoviejo, and went prepared to propose matrimony to the handsome Elena. He had plans to bring her back to Paraiso, but it was obvious to all the family that his young woman was not going to be a farmer's wife!

So Alfonso pitched in, anxious to use his newly-learned skills in a real harvest, and his efforts were appreciated by both the owners-hacendados as well as the field workers, with whom he was very popular.

Pilar tried to stay out of sight, waiting all day for the stolen embraces of her fiancé. A worried Mara had confided in her, and the two spent 'safe' hours in the smaller, Palacios house, where only the old General, unable to hear them, spent his days reading and napping.

Mara, who had always admired Carlos, now became afraid of him, unable to imagine her whole life ahead as his wife!

When Pilar told her of Eduardo's love, and her reciprocation, and of their vows to wait until marriage for intimacy, Mara grew slightly jealous. *This* was 'love' as she had imagined it!

However, the feverish pitch on the hacienda did not last more than a few weeks, when all became calm and routine once more.

The change in the seasons was approaching, and now El Paraiso was prepared.

As the rainy season began, there had been some subtle changes at the plantation.

Eduardo was back on office duty. Felipe had returned from the provincial capital, without a bride, and was again his aide.

Alfonso was staying with the owners of a banana farm in the region, ostensibly to learn the business, but also to see more of the daughter, Susana.

This left Carlos, as before, on his own, to run the day to day business of all their surrounding properties. In the evenings, he was too proud to beg to see Mara, next door, so spent them alone, fuming, and planning his next move.

His mind was more and more concerned with this young blonde beauty, who began to haunt even his sleeping hours!

These thoughts were consuming him, and he saw, in his mind's eye, her long legs, her slim but softly rounded figure and glorious shiny long hair.

In short, he was, unbeknownst to himself, falling in love.

Twenty-one

Eduardo decided, once the torrential rains had almost stopped and the swollen river had become calmer, to take Pilar to Chone for a private marriage. Then he informed his brother, Carlos, who was secretly jealous, but put up a manly front, congratulating him and contributing a large gift to help pay for the trip there and to Bahía for their honeymoon.

He, himself, had also decided to wait no longer. Mara, he reasoned, had had plenty of time now to get used to the idea of marriage. As soon as Eduardo returned, in a month or so, he planned to take his bride to Bahía also.

For two months, he had been in secret negotiations with a cacao trader there to purchase a seaside house. Now that there were trains taking the mail, he could close the transaction in time to make use of the home for his own honeymoon.

Pilar and Mara had spent the last year together, learning to cook with Dela, and to sew, with the hacienda's main seamstress, Nolita. In fact, Pilar had made her own charming wedding dress, complete with lace collar and cuffs, over white satin.

But Mara was not anxious to emulate her best friend's prowess. She realized, more each passing day, that the choice of husband was not to be hers; that she was the choice, not the chooser.

And she knew, too, that her brothers would not always be there to care for her; Felipe was engaged to his Elena, and there was talk of his going into his future father-in-law's banking business in Portoviejo. And Alfonso, also, seemed disposed to leave, since he and Susana Aguilar were now betrothed, and her father had offered him a position in his banana operations.

Now, Carlos and Eduardo would again live as before, without any help in running the main hacienda, and those surrounding it.

The old General, though, decided to remain where he was, and would continue to live in the smaller house with Eduardo and Pilar, while Carlos and Mara, with the children, would live in the larger home.

Of them all, Mara was the only one who was not happy at her future prospects. The laughing, carefree girl of past years seemed to have disappeared, and the fifteen-year-old had become quiet and thoughtful.

Carlos, thinking and dreaming of her during the day, and through the long evenings, made many plans for their future together. He knew now that he would have to win her love, and that he must be very careful not to repulse her.

For a year now, he had spoken to her softly, always with others nearby, and sent her little gifts to show his affection. She had reacted with good manners, but without any reciprocation of feeling. He ached to get a response, even of a smile, but she was withdrawn and serious with him; and he had become her slave!...

The weather had so improved that the nuptials date was set for Eduardo and Pilar, who had shyly postponed it so that her menstrual days would be over first; and they began to gather their belongings for the wedding trip.

A week before their departure, the days began to be very warm, and one afternoon Pilar, now free of her monthly period, asked Mara to go down to the river with her for a cooling swim. But Mara was not feeling well and declined. So Pilar set off by herself.

It was a little after noon, and siesta-time, when all on the hacienda were eating their mid-day meal, or resting. So Pilar felt no one would notice her in the protected grove at the foot of the garden.

She put her bare feet in the water, and decided to enter up to her knees, but her dress became wet. She pulled it up over her head, dipping down into the cool stream. Then, looking around and seeing no one, daringly put her dress and underclothes on a nearby rock, and lay, naked and submerged, eyes closed, totally relaxed.

Suddenly she felt another body close to hers! A hand came up over her mouth and she was pushed into the gravelley streambed, face down; and the man behind her was touching her everywhere!

No part of her body was missed by his free hand, from her hair to her neck, shoulders, back, breasts and thighs, and suddenly he was forcing her down under his weight, and he entered her from behind.

She could not cry out, with her face covered by the large hand, and pushed half into the water. She was in terrible pain, but he would not release her, as he pushed and pushed, again, and again, until her blood ran into the stream.

As suddenly as he had come, he thrust her aside, and the weight lifted from her. Half-blinded and choking from the water, she lifted her head and saw a man disappear into the trees.

She managed to pull herself up, bruised and aching, and found her wet clothes. As she dressed herself, in tears, she noticed something shining on the bank. Climbing up, barefoot still, she saw it was a gold button, and one that she recognized instantly.

The only button like that she had ever seen was on the vest that Don Carlos wore day in and day out, in every season of the year.

Twenty-two

When Pilar reached her house, she was thankful that Eduardo was in his office, and that Mara was probably in her bedroom. Only the General, sound asleep, sat in his rocker, and did not stir as she passed him, barefooted and soaking wet.

She went into her own room, stepped out of her clothing and wrapped a blanket around her cold body. Then, putting a towel beneath her, she sat gingerly on the edge of the bed, afraid to soil it with the blood that covered her inner thighs.

By now, she was past crying, feeling only a deep despair. How could Eduardo love her now!? Should she confide in him? What would happen to their wedding plans?...She couldn't answer her own questions!

The afternoon light began to dim into dusk, and still she sat there, huddled in her blanket. Soon she would be called to the table for the evening cena; she must move before anyone could see her like this!

Painfully, she rose, her legs, pelvis and back aching. She poured water from a pitcher into the basin that sat on a small wash stand, and sponged herself as best she could. When she finished, she dried herself with one of the embroidered towels that hung beneath the table.

Slowly she dressed in dry clothes, and her shivering body began to warm again.

A little later, when Mara knocked softly, Pilar was able to compose her face and meet her friend, saying,

"Is it already time for supper? I'm ready!"

All during the evening meal of sweet banana muffins and hot

chocolate, with left-overs of the midday meal, chicken soup and maní, or ground peanuts, Pilar debated inwardly the wisdom of confiding her shame to Mara. But she realized with certainty that this would be fatal for them both: that Mara could not know what the man who was to be her life's partner had done to her, and that she could not risk how Eduardo might react. The situation was dangerous for all concerned!

Mara had already forgotten that Pilar had gone down to the river, since she herself had lain in bed all day with a severe headache.

And so night came, and the date of the journey to Chone and Bahía had not changed. Pilar and Eduardo were to be married in seven days.

Each day, Pilar expected to have her monthly period, which should have begun the very day of the attack. She and Eduardo had planned their travels around this date. But nothing happened, and now she feared the worst! Indeed, when they left, she was sick with anxiety, especially since they were to meet her parents in Chone, and she would not be able to confide in her mother.

So she bore the secret alone, dreading to know the outcome of this impossible situation.

Twenty-three

Leaving Paraiso was the happiest moment Pilar had had recently. She was entirely joyful to be with her betrothed alone, actually on the way to begin their life together.

As they had finished loading the carriage that was to take them to Chone, Carlos came out of the main house to bid them goodbye, and, for the first time since the encounter at the river, was forced to come face to face with Pilar.

Neither one wanted to see the other, but Eduardo, totally ignorant of the past event, softened the moment, embracing his brother in farewell, while Pilar looked down at her gloved hands.

"Goodbye for now, hermano, and thank you for giving us so much help for this trip! We'll be back, Dios mediante, in three weeks." And added, innocently, "We'll miss you."

As the carriage drew away, Pilar, not looking back directly, managed to wave briefly.

Carlos, seeing his only brother so happy, felt a searing shame spread through him. Had his long-awaited, momentary triumph over Pilar brought him joy?! He agonized over what he had done, that could never be undone! He knew, to the very depths of his soul, that he had ruined purity, and that Mara, equally pure, would never forgive his act, must never know of it!

But, for all his remorse, he feared most to confess his sin! How could he be forgiven, and what would it cost the rest of his life here at Paraiso?

Nevertheless, as the days of the honeymooners' return came ever closer, Carlos realized that, if he were to try to rectify his life and future, he must act soon.

So, one lovely morning, as the bell tolled with a seeming message on the clean air, Carlos faced his inner self with resolve. He would speak to Father Benedicto today!

After the morning rounds, with Pepín at his side, and time spent reviewing Eduardo's neat company books in the office, he sat down to a lonely breakfast, aware that Mara, so close next door, was doing the same.

Then, feeling his will weaken somewhat, he sent a servant-girl to fetch the priest.

Face to face with the serious Father Benedicto, he faltered inwardly.

But he carried on his mission: "Father, buenos días. I hope you are well?

"Buenos días, Don Carlos. Yes, I am well enough; better now, since the weather is a bit cooler…all these clothes, you know!" he added sheepishly, indicating his long, heavy cassock.

"Yes, I know," agreed Carlos. "We would both be better off with less on!"

The formalities over, the priest looked questioningly at his sponsor, a wise expression in his eyes.

"Yes…well…the truth is, Father…I have a need to confess!" There! It was out, at last, the Truth!

The cleric let a veil cover his expression, sad that this proud man must have fallen once more.

"Yes, my son. Let us go into the chapel."

The small space was dim and somewhat cooler than outdoors. As soon as the priest entered his place behind a curtain in the confessional, Carlos sank to his knees on his side of the tiny cubicle.

He made the sign of the cross, and said at once,

"Bless me, Father, for I have sinned"…'"I confess to Almighty God and to you, Father, that I have…I have…;" and here Carlos broke down in tears, and, choking, continued: "I have raped a pure and innocent girl! And I can't go on without repentance…for the rest of my life!" And he sobbed again.

Father Benedicto heard these words with utter surprise and

repugnance, and witnessed his patron's breakdown with deep sorrow.

"It is good for you to cry, my son. You have done irreparable damage to some poor maiden. And you must never do this again! You must remember this confession every time you are tempted in the future!"

Carlos heard and, deeply moved, repeated the same phrases he had learned in boyhood: "I am sorry for these and all the sins of my past life, and I ask pardon of God and penance of you, Father."

"Don Carlos, this may be a sin worse than murder, but if you are truly sorry to the depths of your soul, God will pardon you."

"You must pray each day, morning, noon and night, for celestial guidance and purification. Pray, too, to your patron saint; and pray the rosary at least twice a week."

"If you do these with a pure heart, God will know it...Now, make an act of contrition."

So Carlos began, "O my God, I am heartily sorry for having offended Thee. And I detest all my sins because I dread the loss of Heaven and the pains of Hell, but most of all because they offend Thee, my love. I firmly resolve, with the help of Thy grace, to confess my sins, to do penance and to amend my life. Amen."

With this said, the priest made the sign of the cross, gave him absolution and said, "God bless you. Go in peace."

Twenty-four

Carlos, freed somewhat from his mental anguish, now anticipated the newlyweds' return with a new anxiety. What if Pilar had already confided in Mara?! He had to find out, and make some swift decisions, if necessary.

For the first time in months, he went to the smaller house and knocked. Mara, never imagining it was he, opened the door and stood there, speechless.

Carlos, seeing the beloved of all his secret dreams standing there before him once more, could say nothing for a moment. This vision, with her pale skin, bright blue eyes and golden hair pulled back in a chignon, dazzled him, and he longed to encircle her with his arms, kiss her sweet mouth.

But he said nothing, just gazed with hungry eyes. She was still as a doe, poised to turn and run.

"Mara!" was all he could say at first. The forty-year old man of experience was bewitched by the poised fifteen-year-old girl-woman before him.

"Mara!" he repeated. "May I come in? We need to speak…of our plans."

She said nothing, but stepped aside, opening the door farther.

"Who is it!" called the General. "Did someone knock?"

Carlos stepped inside, and, using the old man as an entrée, walked confidently over to him, to shake his hand and inquire as to his health.

Then, excusing himself, he motioned Mara to a palm-woven couch on the other side of the large sala.

"Mara, my dear, speak to me!"

"Yes…good day…how are you?" she was not sure what she was to call him now.

"My dear one, querida, can't you call me 'Carlos'? I'm yours, you know; for today and always."

"Yes; Carlos." In a sense it was a relief for Mara to be able to speak again; she had been quiet or silent for so many months.

"My dear, we are very soon to be man and wife, and we will be in Chone, and then at the seaside. I hope you will like it!"

"Yes, thank you, I will," she replied, obedient by habit.

"But *really* like it!" he insisted, trying again to tear down the barrier between them.

"I have bought you a cottage in Bahía, so if you like, we can stay there whenever you please!"

Finally, a faint smile appeared, and heartened at this, her took her hand in his, and caressed it.

"I have bought you a ring, too; I hope the correct size! And some pearls for your beautiful throat!"

Now, a little of her past mischievous expression crossed Mara's face, and her smile deepened. She had been so lonely these past months; it felt good to be pampered!

Pilar had been so engrossed with Eduardo that her company had not been able to penetrate her sadness. Lately, though, she had thought, or maybe imagined, that Pilar, too, was more serious and withdrawn than usual. And this had isolated her still further.

Now, suddenly, her youth was reviving, and she felt a surge of optimism about her future. Maybe Carlos was not the aggressive male she had feared. He seemed docile and kind today!

Emboldened by his mildness, she said, somewhat daringly,

"I have no wedding dress, you know! I can sew now, but not *that* well! And there are other things…too…"She stopped, too shy to mention undergarments.

"We'll buy you anything you want…ready-made. And I'll have Nolita make you a beautiful wedding gown from my mother's!"

She was so happy and grateful that she bent to kiss his hand.

Needing no further encouragement, he returned the kiss to her hand and, moving closer, embraced her, kissing her forehead, eyelids and then her lips.

And, for the first time in her life, Mara kissed a man, and let him do what he wished with her mouth...liking it, wanting more!

Twenty-five

By the time Eduardo and Pilar returned to Paraiso, Mara had blossomed into a willing fiancée.

Her change of heart had also altered her speech, her facial expression and her general demeanor. Now her cheeks were rosy once again. She walked with a spring in her step, and her laughter could be heard throughout the day. In short, she was happy that she would very soon be a bride!

The wedding dress was ready and, with its long, puffy folds, would take up a suitcase by itself. Nolita had done a magnificent job of fitting the ample gown to Mara's slender body. She had also made her lacey undergarments and two lovely daytime outfits, inspired by the French magazines that Carlos provided.

Mara was so taken up in these plans and fittings that she hardly noticed Pilar's serious demeanor when she and her new husband returned. The newlyweds were so obviously in love and well-suited to each other, that it was easy to miss this subtle change in the bride. Now, instead of an outgoing happiness, she seemed to have matured overnight into a woman of quiet responsibility.

But the time for departure was drawing near and now Mara could hardly contain her excitement at the thought of leaving this nest that she had known for so many years. The sounds of "Chone" and "Bahía de Caráquez" loomed large before the educated but provincial mind; these places were her "Russia" and "England"!

At last, one lovely June morning, the bell tolled as the sun was rising. All of Paraiso seemed refurbished with the largest flowers, the greenest leaves and the tallest trees against a rosy sky.

The new carriage that Carlos had ordered for the occasion was brought to the main entrance, and all the ribbon-adorned boxes, strapped suitcases and napkin-covered hampers of fresh fruit and panes de yucca were stored in the ample trunk at the rear.

Mara, dressed in one of her new outfits, a floor-length dark blue skirt topped with a matching jacket with puffed sleeves and a lacey white jabot, looked stunningly beautiful. Her lovely face was shaded by a large matching straw hat made of the finest fibers that Jipijapa could provide.

Carlos, looking prosperous in a new suit and tall hat, beamed with pride and happiness. He was in love and about to marry the woman of his dreams!

Eduardo and Pilar, brave at the side of her protector, came to the doorway to wave their goodbyes, the servants standing close behind them to get a peek at the couple. And then the carriage pulled forward, drawn by a pair of matched horses that trotted jauntily down the avenue, now shaded on both sides by giant jacaranda trees.

The first part of the trip was not long. Soon they arrived in Chone, still a small town of unpaved streets and undistinguished buildings. But it was filled with activity and the noises of a small city. Donkeys and horse-drawn vehicles passed mounted riders and handcarts, raising clouds of dust in the streets and along the board sidewalks. A few homes in the Spanish style were intermixed with smaller, nondescript ones, shabby shops alongside larger, glass-fronted ones, open markets and a few large public buildings.

Among the latter was the "Hotel Majestad", where they pulled up, immediately surrounded by half a dozen uniformed bellboys who grappled with each other in an attempt to take the most luggage from the carriage. The manager himself, a rotund individual with a moist red face, came to the top of the entrance steps to greet his expected, illustrious guests.

"Ah, Don Carlos!" he exclaimed. "We are honored to welcome you to our beautiful hotel. All is ready in your rooms!" And turning quickly to watch his employees, ordered, "To number one, and take care with those cases!"

Mara was enchanted with every aspect of this journey! It was the first time she had ever ridden in a bonafide carriage, the first time she had been dressed so like a real lady, and the first time she had seen Chone: the town that was so close to them, but that could have been hundreds of miles from her Pasto or Paraiso! Compared to the quiet activities of the rural lands, this flurry of movement, dust and all, fascinated her! She had longed to descend and walk along the streets, meeting strangers and entering the mysterious doorways of tiny, dimly-lit shops; and visit the teeming marketplace, with all its beckoning, colorful goods hanging with pegs on clotheslines, or offered on long tables for blocks ahead.

But they had whisked past these wonders, and now she must act the part of a world-weary lady, too tired to do anything but wash her hands in the enamel basin provided and lie down for a short siesta.

It was almost too much for Carlos to see his soon-to-be wife lying there, suddenly so close to him, in the same room! He was mad with love for her!

But he left her there, and went to arrange their marriage. This was to take place in a large salon of the hotel, with only a civil servant, a priest and two unknown witnesses to be present. All would be ready in three hours.

So, after ordering fresh flowers for the salon and a special bouquet for his bride, Carlos returned to their rooms. Mara was too excited to rest; she hopped up and accompanied her husband-to-be down to the dining room.

This was a large space, and had been decorated in the taste of the day, with ornate plaster molding, many gold fixtures, soft kerosene lighting and copies of large paintings from Europe. For such a provincial town, it was quite lavish, and many passing politicians and army officers had been attended here.

After a light luncheon, Carlos took Mara back to their rooms, and called a maid to help her change into her wedding dress.

When the manager informed him of the arrival of the priest, he went to meet him in the salon. Minutes later, Mara appeared, a vision of radiant young beauty in her flowing white gown, adorned only by her pearls and the bouquet of colorful flowers.

The two signed the clerk's papers, along with witnesses from the hotel staff, then exchanged vows before the priest, a Father Tobías.

Carlos placed the ring on Mara's finger, not believing that this had finally come about!

So, by five o'clock in the afternoon, the handsome, mature man and his young bride were man and wife! It was real!

Rather than rush upstairs, they returned to the now well-attended dinning room, and all heads turned to see the young bride with her groom, exchanging smiles and nods of approval. The two, not hungry, had only a glass of wine with some cheese. Then, not wanting dinner, they rose and returned to their rooms.

Mara, not shy, asked Carlos to unfasten the twenty tiny buttons that went down the back of her dress; then removed it, matter-of-factly.

Not exactly sure what was expected of her, she continued to take off the rest of her clothes, and was about to put on a new long sleeping gown of silk.

But Carlos, also undressing, put his hand over hers, and said in a husky voice,

"No, Marita…leave it…just stay the way you are."

Suddenly very self-conscious, she slid, naked, under the bed sheets.

Carlos dropped his new clothing onto the floor and followed her, blowing out the kerosene lamp.

He could not grasp the fact that this was not another dream…that Mara was real! He reached out, as if to make sure. He ran his hand over a very real arm, then her waist, and up over the perfect breasts that had only been hinted at in her loose clothes. He was delirious with joy, and pulled her to his chest, his mouth on hers, wanting to devour her.

She, not knowing what exactly to expect, reacted like the healthy young creature she was. This was her new life, this strong, good-looking man, who was claiming her now. She had never felt as she did, suddenly, as if a flame burned through her, reacting to this hands, first on her breasts, then sliding down her body, between her thighs, pushing her legs apart.

And then, for both, the moment erupted into the greatest pleasure either had ever known; and, as she answered his every move, her body and mouth opened wide to receive him.

Twenty-six

Nothing could have properly prepared Mara for her first glimpse of the sea! The newlyweds-of-a-day arrived in Bahía by nightfall, having started off from Chone at dawn. But the Pacific Ocean was clearly visible in the moonlight, calmly rippling toward the shore. Under the stars, Carlos led his bride to the edge of the water so that she could hear the lapping of the waves on the sand, and reach down to touch the salty water. She was totally enchanted, and, holding Carlos' hand, ran along the sandy edge until her fragile shoes gave in.

Laughing, she removed them, and, in stocking feet, skirt held high, walked toward their just-built cottage with her new husband.

Everything Carlos had promised her about the gift-house was true! It had all one could desire, including a sala filled with tropical furniture, all made just up the coast from them, a kitchen with the newest imports that could be found in the local stores and two comfortable bed chambers, with smooth sheets and coverlets, and white gauzy curtains.

Carlos immediately lit kerosene lamps which glowed in the pretty living room. The driver had put all their luggage by the entrance door before taking the horse and carriage to the neighborhood stable.

They opened the hamper and, hungry now, ate a picnic dinner of the remaining good food that Dela had packed. In the morning, a local girl was coming to cook and clean; but for the moment, they were blissfully alone.

Carlos, so used to a rigorous work schedule, was finding it difficult to adjust to lazy hours and sheer happiness. But, just being near Mara was heady medicine, and he could not refrain from touching her, stroking her hair and bending to kiss her, time after time.

After their little supper, they looked at each other with happiness and anticipation in their eyes, and, as one, rose to retire to the bedroom…

Though they would have preferred to keep to themselves, Carlos felt Mara should at least have a glimpse of the town, which was growing quickly.

True, its port was not as deep as its neighbor to the south, Manta, but it accommodated a variety of ships, as well as myriads of tiny to large fishing vessels. And, because of the many foreign boats that stopped here, there was bustling business from the docks to a wide variety of shops selling the incoming merchandise.

They spent a whole morning strolling on the sandy streets, stopping occasionally to order some useful item for Paraiso.

Suddenly, they found themselves face to face with Alberto Granados and his wife Cecilia, their two boys and little daughter, Elena.

Their neighbor, always haughty, tried hard to smile, presented his wife, stared at Mara and said little beyond, "Humm" and "Haww."

They all stood there in the now-hot sun, at the entrance of the store belonging to Señora Cecilia's father, Don José Montenegro.

After being congratulated for their marriage, and exchanging a few words on the weather, the men tipped their straw hats and each party went its separate way.

Carlos, very annoyed with his uncooperative neighbor, led Mara toward the wharves, and they stood admiring a docking ship, flying an English flag.

As they approached the hustle and bustle of the piers, the ship's officers were just coming down the gangplank, and one of them looked very familiar.

Sure enough, Carlos recognized Joshua Crowley, in the starched white uniform of the British Merchant Marines, now sporting Captain's stripes. He saw them at the same moment, walked up to the couple, and, with a friendly smile, saluted them, glancing questioningly at Mara.

"Hóla, mi amigo! Don Carlos, what bring you here to Bahía? Is this señorita a relative?"

Carlos laughed and presented his bride, "María Margarita.

PARAISO

Perhaps you hadn't heard? My first wife died four years ago. This is her sister."

"Mara!?" asked Crowley. "Can this be the little girl at the wedding I attended at Paraiso?!"

"Yes," agreed Carlos, "It is!" And Mara smiled up at him, liking his laughing eyes.

The three talked for a few minutes, then decided to continue the conversation in a shadier place, and walked toward an outdoor, beach-front restaurant specializing in 'cebiche de camarones', a shrimp cocktail made in their own regional way.

The two men continued to speak; of the war in Europe, Crowley's consequent adventures at sea and the record-high sales of cacao in foreign markets.

Mara was fast being initiated into the life of a Latin American wife, which usually demanded docile silence. But smiles and nods of a golden head went a long way, and she didn't really feel left out.

In fact, after this one day of intermingling, Mara was so content with the absolute privacy at their beach-front home that she yearned to stay longer.

Carlos indulged her for two weeks, then softly reasoned, 'I must return, linda mía. We can't leave the hacienda without its chief. Poor Eduardo can't be in two or three places at once."

"Yes, my husband. I know you're right, yet this is so lovely. I will miss the water so!"

"I know, I know." As they spoke, he cradled her in his arms, stroking her hair. He had not thought he could love her more, but each day his feelings seemed to double, until he thought he would burst with amor!

And she, too, seemed to adore and revere him increasingly, so that he felt like a monarch with his queen!

Finally, though, they had to put their clothing back into the suitcases, refill the hamper with fresh fruits, new empanadas, and bottles of water.

The carriage came around to the entrance as the sun came up, and they, dressed for travel, entered it together, to return to their old life once more.

Twenty-seven

By the time the rainy season began in December, it was obvious to the whole household that Pilar was expecting a baby.

Mara, excited for her friend, started taking her sewing lessons seriously, and, with the help of Nolita, she made one camisón after another! These little shirts were then embroidered, and further enhanced with lace ruffles.

Pilar was appreciative, but was calm and remote from all these preparations. Eduardo, though, was excited and proud. At last, at thirty-five, he was to become a father, perhaps have a son!

This season was particularly oppressive: day after day of drenching rains, flattening the plants and pushing down the leaves and branches, from the high canopy of palo prietos protecting the groves, to the cacao trees themselves. The winds were so fierce at times that they knocked even the bean pods growing up the trunks down into the soggy, decaying leaf litter below. The mild, shallow river of the dry season became a wild torrent of whitecaps, pushing aside all in its way, leaving the banks covered with debris.

The days and nights grew oppressively hot and muggy, and put everyone in a gray mood. Carlos was forced to work in these conditions, side by side with his employees, his boots covered to the ankles with mud and soggy plants. Eduardo continued his part in the office, but often joined his brother, as one crisis followed another.

The young brides often ate their meals alone, as the working hours of the men became more erratic. And, even they, best friends as they were, were quiet and serious together.

At times, it seemed this muggy season would never end, and that their Paraiso had somehow been washed away and had disappeared. One day, though, only dripping from the roof and outbuildings was witness to the past few months of unusual rainfall, and the sun emerged to begin the drying out of land and souls alike. While everyone rejoiced to see signs of a coming dry and cooler period, only Pilar, now very large, and expecting to deliver in about a month, remained passive. She was burdened by the thought of this child of an unloved, even hated 'father', and with each succeeding day found it harder and harder to keep her burden to herself.

Several times she was on the brink of confiding in Mara, but she stopped herself, knowing that the information would probably kill their friendship and the other's marriage. But her wild thoughts, so carefully hidden by her demeanor, were gnawing away at her mental balance, and she spent ever more time alone.

Her husband, also, was worried. His sweet, affectionate wife was becoming more remote daily; and he, not knowing the source of her unfamiliar gravity, felt that he was losing his life!

At last, one day in early February, Pilar, now very big and expecting her child at any time, crossed the short space between houses and entered the dimly lit little chapel next door. She had observed this outside entrance for many days now, and knew that Father Benedicto entered there daily at this hour.

And this day, too, the priest knelt, alone, at the tiny altar, silently praying. He turned, though, when he heard footsteps behind him, and gazed with a puzzled expression at Pilar.

No sooner had he greeted her, than the poor girl sat down on the nearest bench and began to sob. The priest was even more perplexed now! This young woman and Mara were punctilious in coming to confession and communion, and neither had ever spoken of a single mortal sin! What could make this lady cry so, at a time when she should be anticipating the happiest moment of her life?!

"Father!" she burst out, after calming down somewhat; and, using her handkerchief, said, in a muffled voice,

"I have such a problem! Please help me, help me!"

"Yes, my daughter, I will; just tell me what's troubling you!"

"Oh, Father, the worst thing! Please let God forgive me!"

"Yes, hija, daughter, go on! *What* is this trouble?"

And then, amidst more tears and sobs, Pilar let the dam break! She told him of the sin against her, and that this aggressor was the true father of the child she was to bear!

She went on to say, firmly now, that she did not want to raise this baby, and planned to give it away! Still she did not mention Carlos' name.

"But why?" asked the frowning priest. "This is not natural or right! Who is this man!?" he demanded.

"I can't say his name, ever!" answered Pilar. "but I know it is better this way!"

The two talked for an hour, Pilar revealing that Julia, a pretty servant girl who had been living with them in the smaller house, had already agreed to take the child away, and raise it as her own!

"But how can you explain its disappearance to your husband?" asked the flabbergasted priest.

"I have a plan, Father. When it is born, Dulce, our nurse, can accompany her, very early or very late, and stay with her for the first month or so."

"Where would they go? Not near here!"

"No, Father, to Bahía. I am going to ask Doña Mara if they could stay in their house there. She will know, too, about the baby's father, but not his name! Just that he works here!"

The poor priest was dumbfounded at all this prearranged intrigue.

"But what will your husband think, when his new child disappears?!" he demanded.

"He will only know that it died!" continued Pilar. "We will have a funeral...with an empty, closed casket...to spare him! That is where I most need your help Father!" and Pilar searched his face for an answer, anxious and tearful.

The priest rose abruptly, and walked away from her.

"This is outrageous! Never in my life have I heard such an un-Christian proposal! This is utterly impossible!" He paused a moment, his hands covering his anguished face.

"There is no reason to do this! Who is this man who defiled you!? If you don't tell me this, I'll listen no further!"

"Don Carlos!" Pilar whispered, and buried her face in her hands. The priest, overcome, sat down abruptly.

"!Dios mío! My God!"

Twenty-eight

A full yellow moon hung over Paraiso that late February night. The crisp dark sky was sprinkled with twinkling stars, and a brisk breeze from the coast blew over the waving trees.

All the lights gleamed from the windows of the two houses; maid servants ran to and fro carrying linens and basins of hot water.

Suddenly, a cry pierced the night, and the muffled sound of another followed. The old nurse, Dulce, stood by Pilar's bed, not allowing anyone near. Everyone but Julia, the young maid, was sent away, and the door was shut. Even the father, Eduardo, was told to wait.

He was in a panic, not knowing what had happened, wanting to enter their bedroom and take Pilar in his arms, see his child. Was it a boy or girl? He was frantic, and knocked imperatively on the door.

"Dulce, open immediately! What is going on?!"

From the other side, Dulce called,

"Yes, sir. Just a moment. I'm coming."

But she didn't come at once. There were shuffling noises from the other side.

Just as Eduardo was ready to break down the door, Carlos came up to him put an arm around his brother and led him away.

"Patience, hermano. You can go in as soon as they clean things up a bit. Come, sit down with me!"

Suddenly, the bedroom door opened and Dulce's head appeared.

"Don Eduardo! Come in, please!" but she held her finger up to her lips, adding,

"Please be very quiet, sir; the baby is not well!"

"What!? What do you mean?!" and he pushed past her, striding across the room toward the large brass bed.

There was Pilar, pale but beautiful, her long black hair flowing over the white pillows. Julia stood next to her, holding a blanket-covered little figure.

He swooped down to enfold his young wife in his arms, almost forgetting the baby. But, after kissing her gently, and murmuring words of love, he looked around to find the child.

"Well?" he demanded. "Do I have a boy or a girl?"

Dulce stood like a buffer between him and Julia, but said in a low, sad voice,

"It's a boy, sir, but he's not very well," and, turning to the maid, said, "Julia, let the father see his son!'

Eduardo, now panicking, looked fearfully at the bundle in her arms. The baby looked all right to him, maybe a little pale; but he was very still.

"What's the matter, Dulce? Why isn't the doctor here?"

"He was here, sir. But he went to rest a few hours ago, and I said I'd send for him. But this was very sudden, and I didn't have a chance."

By this time, Carlos was at the door, taking in the scene, and immediately sent a servant to fetch Dr. Cueva from the other house.

The truth of the matter was that Father Benedicto had suggested that the doctor retire early, and leave him to keep the late night vigil. He had not wanted to reveal the devious plans of the women.

For now, Mara, too, knew of Pilar's plight, and, not knowing the identity of the real father, had immediately agreed to help her.

By the time the doctor arrived, the baby was crying, and they passed him to Pilar to nurse. Dr. Cueva, looking into the room, saw a reassuring scene, and waited outside in the sala with the two brothers.

It was now after midnight, and everyone was exhausted from the long hours of waiting. The doctor had examined Pilar, and found her in a normal condition; and the baby, though perhaps a little anemic and quiet, seemed otherwise all right.

Eduardo kissed his wife, who lay with her eyes closed, patted the blanket covering the baby, and tiptoed from the room.

All the men, except the priest, now left, to sleep in the big house.

The moment all was quiet again, there was a flurry of activity in the room. The nurse, Dulce, head covered with a dark shawl, carried the tiny bundle, and Julia followed her outside.

The priest accompanied them, walking, with only the moonlight to guide them toward the workers' houses. There, in the road, a small horse-drawn wagon was waiting: with a few cushions and blankets inside, along with a large covered basket of food.

Father Benedicto helped the two women and baby into the cart, whispered directions to the young driver, giving him some money, and made the sign of the cross over them all, saying in a soft voice, "May God protect you!"

Then the cart started quietly down the wind-swept road, heading to the west, out of Paraiso.

Lifting his long robe in order to walk faster, the priest hurried back to the smaller house, praying all the while for the travelers, the young mother, and all involved in this impossible plot, including himself!

By now, all the lights were out, and even the sky was darker, the night air cold. Outside the entrance door of the house, he reached under a large hibiscus bush, pulling out a small object. Then, looking guiltily around and seeing no one, he entered the house and went straight to the main bedroom.

Pilar was now wide awake, and sat up, nervously, in bed, waiting. No one else was in the room.

He held up his hand for silence, and put the long box on the floor by the bed. It had been painted white and nailed shut. It was the coffin for the newborn, and Father Benedicto blessed it, and wished with all his heart for this day to end.

Twenty-nine

Shortly after dawn, Paraiso's bell tolled, sending the sound far out on the clean, dry air. Somewhere, a cock crowed.

Slowly, the daily activities began, as the still sleepy house servants began their tasks. The men of the house, too, were unusually tired from yesterday's events, and were late to arise.

Eduardo was the last to join his brother and Dr. Cueva, badly dressed and unshaven. The two priests, who usually had their meals apart from the others, joined them in the dining room, though they remained standing while morning greetings were quietly exchanged.

Father Benedicto said softly,

"If you wish, I can see the Señora Pilar this morning. Perhaps the Señor Doctor will accompany me?"

Unbeknownst to the others, the priest had never retired! He had spent the hour or so before daybreak praying, asking the Lord for help in this terrible time.

Then, as dawn approached, he hurriedly walked to the servants' quarters in search of substitutes for Dulce and Julia. The nurse had given him the names of two experienced and willing young women, and he asked for them at the door. As promised, the two girls appeared, dressed and ready to accompany him.

Now, with the poor doctor, who had not had time to finish breakfast, Father Benedicto left the room and walked the short distance to the neighboring house.

There, all was unusually quiet, with no one in sight. In the living room, the priest lay his hand on the doctor's arm, stopping him.

"Dr. Cueva, sir...," the priest began. "Very late last night...or, rather, in the early hours of the day…well…you had all left, and I turned to give my blessing to the mother and child, but…well…I'm sad to say this…but…the baby died!" And he made the sign of the cross, inwardly praying hard. "Forgive me, Lord, for this terrible untruth; punish me, if you will, but please, Lord, let the poor Señora be saved!"

The doctor, mouth wide open, stared at him in amazement. "What!? Let me see the infant!" and he began to walk toward the bedroom.

"Doctor! Wait!" said the priest. "Let me finish!"

"Finish?! What more can you say?" and the doctor's face began to redden in anger and frustration.

"That baby was just fine a few hours ago!"

"Yes, but…well…he suddenly turned blue, and stopped breathing, Doctor! The Señora Pilar was in a bad state, and told me not to call you or her husband. She was afraid to have Don Eduardo see him that way! So…so…she asked me to get him ready for burial, quickly…it was such a sad sight!"

"My God!" fumed the frustrated doctor. "What now?! You'll have him in a coffin next!" and he strode towards the bedroom, shrugging off Father Benedicto, who tried in vain to restrain him.

Pilar, who had heard the raised voices, was sitting up in bed, uncombed and red-eyed, when the doctor burst in.

The first thing he saw was the tiny casket. He walked over to it, ignoring the mother, intent on examining the baby. As he tried in vain to open the small box, he exclaimed angrily,

"My Lord in Heaven, this is outrageous! What is going on here!? I demand to see the child!"

"What child?" said a deep voice behind him. "*My* child?!" It was a disheveled Eduardo, who had followed them here.

"What is going on? Pilar, what is that box?!" He knew in his heart, but would not allow such an abominable thought to become fact.

On seeing her husband, Pilar burst into tears, and, sobbing, put her arms out to him.

"Oh, Eduardo, 'Walo' my love, come and comfort me! Our baby is gone!" ("Not a lie," she thought).

He could not ignore her plea, and went over to their bed and held her close.

"You are over-tired, my love. Our baby is fine."

"No, mi amor, his soul is no longer here; his little body is there!" and she pointed downward.

He took in the object on the floor, but at first his mind didn't grasp the significance of it. Just as suddenly, though, he realized what she meant, and, sobbing, held his wife close.

The doctor and priest, in unison, lifted the tiny burden, and left the room together.

Thirty

Eduardo sat with his head in his hands, sick with grief and anger. Father Benedicto and Dr. Cueva had spoken with him, together, as soon as he had arisen. Now, they offered the saddened father a large hot café con leche, which he drank only when urged by the pair of conspirators.

For, earlier, the priest had convinced the younger physician that the speedier the burial, and the putting of the awful reminder of the coffin out of sight, the better. Now, with guilty consciences, the two awaited their younger employer's decision.

At this point, Carlos came into the dining room, looking around at the serious faces.

"What is going on?! he demanded, now worried at seeing his brother so sad.

Father Benedicto answered, "Buenos días, Don Carlos! We were just about to make a decision."

"And what decision was that!?"

At this point Fernando Cueva spoke up.

"The decision, Don Carlos, to have the funeral this morning, for little Eduardo Luis."

"Eduardo Luis!!!?" questioned Carlos, amazed.

"And who named the baby, and how was he baptized?! And where is he at present!? What is happening here?!"

Terribly worried now at the very probable exposure of the whole convoluted plan, Father Benedicto rose up, and, with a façade of reasonable cleric, said,

"Don Carlos...Don Eduardo...you know we both, the doctor and

I, (and Father Juan, too, of course), are here at your behest, and with the sole purpose of making your life here at Paraiso easier. Therefore, last night, when all was so sudden, and even tragic, we were forced to make a quick decision."

Here, he failed to mention that the doctor was not part of "we," the late night before.

Then he went on"…So, my Señores, we just smoothed the way for this sad necessity." And continued,

"As to the baptism, when I saw the signs of rapid deterioration in the tiny one's health, I gave him the last rites, and the name of 'Eduardo Luis', as the mother dictated."

Totally exhausted, the priest, now having added new strands in this web of deceit, simply sat down, covered his face with his hands and prayed…that this terrible series of events would pass, realizing with certainty that he would have to leave this place!

This last show of remorse, which passed for saintliness, convinced at least Carlos that it was probably best to get the sad events behind them. Eduardo, completely listless, sorrowfully agreed.

Therefore, at eleven that morning, the four men, some of the house servants, and a few garden workers, gathered at the family cemetery on a small rise behind the main grounds. The mother did not attend.

Father Juan Bautista conducted the short service, and the tiny casket was lowered into the ground, covered over, then blanketed with a small hill of flowers…

Late that night, Father Benedicto disappeared into the darkness on the way to a monastery.

Thirty-one

As every other major event that had occurred at Paraiso, the birth and death of the hacendado's infant had a rippling effect over the lives of the plantation's inhabitants.

Eduardo, himself, did not at once go back to being the loving, attentive husband he had been before the birth of his son. For weeks afterward, he stayed on in his former rooms of the main house, hardly visiting Pilar at all. In his heart of hearts he blamed her for the loss. Somehow, he didn't know how, he felt he had been manipulated and cheated.

The one man he could have confided in, Father Benedicto Romero, had 'disappeared' the night of the funeral, leaving only a long letter of apology to the two brothers. He felt, with certainty, that this wise priest held the key to the puzzle he was passively trying to solve.

Pilar, though now feeling almost physically normal again, was feeling also deeply sorrowful, repentant and neglected. For a few weeks, her mother's milk, stimulated by the first and only feeding of the baby, kept her breasts full and painful; but the milk gradually dried up, as Benita, her faithful personal maid, controlled her diet with special Indian herbs.

But, as her body revived, her low morale kept her in a permanent sad state. The few times her husband visited her, he noticed that the normally beautiful woman was dressed carelessly, her hair in disarray. He did not kiss or touch her; she showed no interest in him.

So they continued apart; he, working longer and longer hours in his office retreat; she, spending her days in semi-solitude, mostly wrestling with her conscience.

But Mara visited her daily, trying to be cheerful and positive. Only when she was sure they were alone, the General in his room, or having a solitary meal, did they discuss their 'plan'.

Mara had spoken to Pablo, the young worker who had driven the 'fugitives' to Bahía. By the time he returned with the 'borrowed' wagon and horse, in the midst of the turmoil in the days following the 'death' of the baby, no one seemed to notice.

So the young conspirators felt they were 'safe'. Pablo had reported to Mara that the new occupants were comfortably installed in the beach cottage, and that the baby was healthy and taking to cow's milk.

But Pilar could not be comforted; her husband had had an heir, and lost him! Now, she would have to pay for this 'crime' for long years to come!

Mara badly missed the wise counsel of Father Benedicto, knowing that Father Juan Bautista, good soul that he was, would not be able to advise or console them in their new predicament.

So the two women, the lonely conspirators, were left with the consequences of their daring plan, that had both succeeded and failed!

Carlos also felt he was losing Mara. She was still loving and demonstrative with him, but he sensed a widening gulf between them. She avoided speaking of the subject that most concerned him these days, and he worried, alone, about his brother's growing melancholy and aloofness.

The demands of the hacienda's chief crop—cacao—kept Carlos occupied for longer and longer hours; either on Paraiso's two-thousand hectares of groves, or in almost daily visits to one or another of their contiguous haciendas, with crops of rubber and coffee. It was not unusual for him to miss the main meal at midday, arriving tired and preoccupied late in the day, with only time and energy to bathe and eat a solitary cena.

His little sons only rarely saw their Papá these days, and depended solely on Mara for a parent's love and guidance. They were growing so fast, and seemed to change daily, leaving babyhood behind.

The older, Eduardo, called 'Walo' as a small child, was now seven and resented the childish 'nick-name'; so they began to address him as Eduardito, which he accepted for the time being. This proud little boy was a small copy of his father... fair, with light brown hair and pale blue eyes.

Jaimito, at five, was a lamb, and cared only to be cuddled and told stories. He was so like Mariana that it hurt and pleased both the father and the aunt/stepmother to see him, with his black hair, ivory skin and laughing green eyes.

The effects of the strange birth and 'death' on the hacienda did not stop at the main houses.

The workers, not having access to other pastimes, relied for their social life on 'stories', either from folktales passed down from generation to generation, often in a mixture of Quechua and old Spanish; or 'secrets', both their own and those of the 'grand people' of their circumscribed world.

As word of mouth spread, field workers and house servants alike reveled in the unusual 'facts' of the birth of Pilar's baby, the midnight disappearance of Father Benedicto, the disappearance and reappearance of an exhausted and almost-lame horse, and, best of all, the sudden funeral of the new infant!

Anyone having had the remotest connection to those events became the centers of their leisure hours; so that Pablo, who had been so discreet, was questioned repeatedly, even though he remained tight-lipped and monosyllabic, not deigning to answer their ceaseless prodding questions.

Benita, too, was labeled a 'traitor' for not divulging any facts about her mistress. And everyone had comments and judgments on the whereabouts of old Dulce and young Julia, the pretty maid from nearby Ricaurte.

So such, with the dry season flying past, was the state of affairs on Paraiso.

Thirty-two

One afternoon, Eduardo, sorely missing his until-recently 'perfect' life, rose from his desk, and decided to visit Pilar, aching to have her back.

He knocked on the familiar door and heard the old General call, "!Pase! Come in!"

The house seemed ominously empty.

"Where is Pilar?!" he asked, looking around and seeing no sign of her.

"Pilar?" said the old gentleman. "Why, she left this morning to stay with her parents! I thought *you* would take her!"

"No," faltered Eduardo. "She didn't come to the office...how did she travel...by horseback?"

"I don't believe so, sir. There was talk of a carriage."

"Thank you," muttered Eduardo, as he turned on his heel and left.

Seeing Mara at the chapel door, he called,

"Mara, have you seen Pilar?!"

"Yes, Eduardo, she left more than an hour ago in the small carriage. Pablo helped her with her bags, and drove her 'home' himself.

Eduardo, completely crestfallen, entered his office and put his head down on the desk.

How could this be!? He had lost his wife!

When Carlos returned from the field late that afternoon, he found a forlorn brother waiting for him.

"I don't understand!" he said, tears welling in his eyes. "What have I done? What happened to our 'eternal love'?!"

Carlos, so tired he could barely stand, put his arm around his brother, saying,

"Hermano, don't worry! Of course she loves you! This is just a reaction to the tension of these past days! She has just lost her first baby! Tomorrow, go to 'San Rafael' to see her; she's your wife—claim her!"

Mara was waiting for Carlos in their bedroom. A basin of steaming hot water sat on the toilette table, and a large tin tub in the middle of the room was filled with more.

She helped him undress, and gently washed every part of him with a fragrant soap. Then she dried him and gave him his nightclothes.

A delicious hot meal was brought to their room, and she sat next to him as he devoured it hungrily. When he had finished, she guided him to their bed, and sat beside it, holding his hand.

"Carlos, mi amor, just lie there and listen. I have a story to tell you."

And she told him that Pilar had been violated by an unknown man, before her marriage, and that the child was his. Since she could not raise the result of such a repugnant act, she had been almost relieved when the baby had not lived!...

Carlos lay still, suddenly understanding the past days.

Thirty-three

Every bone and muscle ached! Carlos, for the first time in his life, did not rise with the tolling of the bell! He lay there, lost in thoughts of past deeds, and the real possibility of eternal Hell!!

Then he felt Mara stir beside him, and turned to see her sweet face, a strand of her long blonde hair across it. He leaned over and carefully lifted the lock, kissing her gently on the lips.

Her eyes opened sleepily, and she smiled under the pressure of his kiss, answering it hungrily. In a moment, they were both aroused, and were embracing, rocking together, both filling a deep need.

Carlos' aches seemed to vanish as they reached a climax together and lay quietly in each other's arms, satisfied for a long moment, before they began to move again.

Later, flushed and fulfilled, they rose to wash and dress together.

Carlos fumbled with the long row of buttons at the back of Mara's long cotton day-dress; then Mara straightened his collar and fastened his vest buttons, noting again that the lowest one was missing.

"Mijito, darling," she said, standing on tip-toe to kiss her husband's chin. "Every day I've been meaning to sew on your button, then forget it! Where is it? I'll do it before breakfast!"

Carlos straightened with alarm! His button! He, too, wondered where it was!

"Don't worry, my darling girl. It'll show up. And I really don't need it!"

Then he crushed her to him, never getting enough of this sweet angel God had sent him!

"Shall we skip breakfast?" he asked wickedly.

"We've had it!" she replied mischievously.

"But let's have a second one...no, Carlos...a 'real' one!"...as he had readily accepted her first offer, and was pushing her toward the bed.

But Mara pushed back softly, and they descended to the dining room.

A gloomy Eduardo was just rising from his first meal of the day.

"Good morning! Stay and keep us company, ñaño," offered Carlos; but Eduardo kept walking, saying,

"Buenos días Mara and Ñaño. No thanks. I want to work a few hours before I ride over to 'San Rafael'.

Mara and Carlos exchanged glances, and she said,

"What a good idea! I'm sure Pilar is very anxious to see you! Please give her our love!"

He nodded and disappeared into the office, closing the door behind him.

"Carlos," started Mara as she drank a glass of fresh orange juice.

"I've been thinking about our little house in Bahía. I'd like to check on it, to make sure it's all right. I know you're too busy to leave right now, but may I go? I can take Benita along, just for a few days...maybe a week?"

Carlos, appearing strong, refreshed and relaxed, did not know if he could possibly last that long without her.

"A whole week, querida?! It's very far for you to travel alone! Let me think about it." And added,

"I'm sure the house is fine; we do have caretakers!"

Mara knew when to stop, and she knew her husband. So she began to plan a trip!...

Before the midday meal, Eduardo was seen cantering down the road, headed towards the west. All during the short ride to 'San Rafael', he worried about how to approach his wife. He felt sure, through his misery, that she loved him, just as he adored her! But she had suffered these last weeks, and *he* had felt ignored, left out of her life.

Now, approaching the Gallardo house, he sent up a fervent prayer that someone in Heaven would give him the right words to say in order to get the right answers!

The gelding, Homero, slowed down as they entered a pretty garden area, and Eduardo dismounted, handing the reins to a young Indian boy who had approached shyly.

"Toma, here," he said. "Where are the señores dueños, the owners?"

"The Señor is in the grove, but the Señora madre and the daughter are inside, sir." And he walked the horse toward a nearby open stable.

Eduardo knocked at the main entrance, and when the door opened, there was Pilar, pale but beautiful.

"My darling!" he cried, throwing caution to the winds, folding her in his arms.

Pilar had had no chance to answer, but did not resist the embrace, and flung her arms around his neck. Their lips met, and the two stood as one, never wanting to let go again.

"Ah, Don Eduardo!" exclaimed his mother-in-law, Otavia.

"How nice of you to come so soon! Pilar has missed you!"

The three entered the main 'sala', and sat there in the cool air, drinking fruit juices, and eating little empanadas filled with various meat pastes.

By mid-afternoon, Pilar had gathered her possessions, and was ready to ride back with her husband; eager to start married life anew!

Thirty-four

It had been raining for two weeks, almost without pause, and it was so warm that a steamy vapor could be seen rising from the sodden earth.

Mara, nervous and impatient, paced from one room to another in the big house. All had been ready for her trip to Bahía when the first of a series of storms came blowing through the plantation, lifting off a few of the less sturdy roofs, sending palm fronds flying, and flattening a few of the stilted, thatched or zinc-roofed huts.

Carlos and Eduardo did not even consider working outside. Only a few of the workers ventured out to clean up the latest batch of refuse, before racing back to their quarters. It was as though they were all being held prisoners with no reprieve, as one storm system followed another.

Then, early one morning, as the bell's tolling echoed out over the sodden acres, the sun's rays pushed the curtains of rain aside, and all the hacienda was bathed in their warm glow.

"Mara, my darling, you can't possibly travel now!"

Carlos was trying to reason with his young, impatient wife.

"Besides, if you did, you'd sink into the deep mud! Wait for the sun to dry things up!" and he kissed her, happy that she couldn't leave.

He and Eduardo were dressed to venture out for the first time in almost three weeks, to inspect the precious cacao groves for damage, and to help clean up the jungle floor. Any fallen pods would either have to be thrown away, if rotted, or rescued and processed at once.

In spite of the unaccustomed disarray of Paraiso's landscape, the sun gave everyone, the 'jefes', or 'chiefs' and workers alike, a feeling of power and the desire to re-order their universe.

Soon the dry season would begin, and this devastation would be but a forgotten nightmare in their day-world of harmony.

But Mara was not to be put off. She ordered picnic food for their trip, added and subtracted from her already packed suitcases, and spoke to the domestic staff of their tasks during her absence.

She had already advised Señorita Mendoza-Rosa, the housekeeper, to send for a suitable girl from Chone, as soon as the weather permitted. She could replace Pilar's present maid, for Mara wished Benita, the discreet one, to accompany her to Bahía.

There was time enough, as it happened, since it would be a week before anyone could come to, or go from Paraiso. No one could remember such a ferocious ending to the winter season! But this land was quick to reassert itself! As the heat of the sun nourished all life, it seemed to give birth to the most outrageously painted flowers, the most gorgeously patterned iridescent butterflies, birds of all sizes and vivid colors; and the most amazing variety of animals: from tiny monkeys, cacao-marauding squirrels, pumas, jaguars, foxes, deer and nutria, among myriad others roaming the jungle.

And now the cacao trees, hiding under their canopy of giant shade trees, had surviving pods that were flowering, too, in their first colors of green and reddish violet, that would later turn to yellow or orange when ready to be picked, with their sweet and fragrant beans inside, just waiting to be found.

****

Amid all this natural abundance came an unexpected rumor!

Ever since Pilar's baby had 'died', Dr. Fernando Cueva, not part of the 'plot', but sensing something unusual occurring, had become more and more distressed and unhappy in this environment. He felt useless, unnecessary and unwanted at Paraiso, and tried to communicate this to the dueños/owners. They, though, were equally in the dark, and preoccupied with their problems, so that they 'heard' him without hearing.

Finally, the poor doctor packed his bags, bid them all goodbye, and boarded a small boat, going down-river, with only one plantation worker, Clodomeo, to guide him as far as Chone.

He had been valued as a companion and healer while on the hacienda, but, once gone, he was soon forgotten amidst all the preoccupations of the days following the 'funeral'.

But the first storm had descended and the boatman from Paraiso had not returned. Had he deserted his usual post? Had he just decided to remain in Chone? No one knew for sure, but, as certain as was the coming of the welcome dry season, was the spreading of the rumor of a capsized boat, and the disappearance of both the oarsman and his passenger, the good Dr. Fernando Cueva.

Ernesto Cucalón, Paraiso's overseer, also heard the rumor, and decided to put it to good use!

Thirty-five

At last the sunny day arrived when Mara was finally given her husband's permission to leave for the coast. She was all smiles amid the hustle and bustle of getting her many packages, baskets and suitcases into the carriage standing at the entrance door of the main house.

Her vigilant husband oversaw the whole process, making sure his 'treasure' had everything she needed for a two weeks' stay. Just before she climbed up into the coach, he reached into his vest pocket, and extracted a large envelope.

"Here are your train tickets, my darling. Put this into your handbag and be very vigilant. There are return tickets, also."

She smiled her happiest smile, returning his embrace and kissing him near the moustache, which, tickling her, made her laugh aloud.

"Goodbye, my darling husband. Yes, I'll be careful…now, where is that Benita!?"

"Here I am, Señora Mara! all ready…my bag is in the carriage."

So the two young women mounted the steps and entered the small vehicle; and, as Pablo snapped his switch, the horse pulled forward, and they moved down the road toward Chone…

After several inquiries, they found the train station in Chone, and its one car reserved for passengers only. Pablo settled them in their seats, piling all their baggage around them, and departed, with best wishes for a safe trip.

This section was only half full, mostly with women and several babies, though a few men were already seated in the long car.

Mara was cheerful and excited, enjoying the noisy activity of this unaccustomed world.

111

From the thrilling preliminary puffs, chugs and rising steam, to the sudden lurches, gathering of speed, then smooth rolling of the heavy train out of the station into the countryside, Mara was enchanted.

She hardly looked away from the large window for the rest of the trip, fascinated by the contrast of this open panorama with the enclosed life of a jungle-surrounded plantation.

The closer they came to the coast, the more the scenery opened up. As they neared their destination, houses appeared with greater frequency. All were typical tropical houses; most built on high stilts, roofed with grass or palm thatch, or zinc; the windows wide and shuttered.

Giant ceibo trees, covered with their white puffs of cotton-wool balls, were scattered over the countryside, along with violet-flowering jacarandas and pink-covered hibiscus bushes, tall as trees.

When, at last, Bahía was near, it was evident, even in the enclosed train compartments, where the salty sea air penetrated and refreshed the travelers.

Mara and an excited Benita stepped down to the station platform counting their various bags and parcels. Many willing laborers rushed up to vie for their business, one persistent young man finally gaining their trust. He then piled all their belongings onto his hand-cart, and followed the two young women through the station and out to the sidewalk. There, another pushing and shoving crowd of cabbies jostled for their trade.

At last, they were settled in an enclosed cab behind an old man and his white mare, trotting down the sandy street toward the beach cottage and the sea.

Thirty-six

Seeing the sea again seemed to revive a hidden longing in Mara; a restless feeling she could not identify. But its beauty filled her with happiness, and she knew, in the deepest part of her seventeen-year-old being, that this immense body of water, with its continual pushing and pulling, was, somehow, her future!

When she and Benita arrived at the cottage door, and it was opened by Dulce, it seemed that years had passed, instead of two months, since they had been together!

While the three stood embracing and chatting, the cab driver unloaded their goods, then waited for his fare, wiping his forehead with a large red bandana.

"Oh, here!" said Mara, finally noticing him. She handed him several coins more than he had asked for, and, bowing and smiling he mounted the cab and drove away.

When the women entered the house, they grew silent, Mara's eyes searching for the baby. Julia sat in a rocking chair by a window, holding a small bundle, and motioned them to approach. Smilingly, she offered her hand to Mara, and pulled back the blanket so that she could view the little face of the sleeping child.

Mara was enchanted, thankful that, for all his unwelcoming entrance to this world, and subsequent difficult flight in the night, he was well and seemingly unaware of his rejection.

At that moment, as if sensing that this was an important meeting, little Eduardo Luis opened his eyes and smiled straight at Mara!

He was so handsome, she thought, and, she held her breath an instant, his eyes were a familiar pale blue! His small thatch of hair was a light brown, with touches of gold, his skin a velvety ivory and pink. What a beautiful baby, with his little jutting chin and small carved features!

"Oh, may I hold him!?" And Julia lifted him toward Mara, who carried him to a nearby chair. He was so warm and sweet! She lowered her face to kiss his forehead, and he smiled again.

Dulce, observing, said,

"That's his second smile! They almost never do that this young. He knows his aunt loves him!"

And Mara promised herself that moment that she would never desert this child; that she would always protect him, keep him safe!

Aloud, though, she said, "We have to look for another house today!"

When the other three, Julia, Dulce and Benita stared at her uncomprehendingly, she went on,

"It's not safe here! After all, it's Don Carlos' house, and he might come at any time. He thinks the cottage is empty, with only Clara and Jorge here to keep it safe and clean. How could we explain three persons living here, and one a little baby?" No, we have to empty this place; today, if possible!"

It was only then that the travelers removed their hats and gloves, and refreshed themselves. Then Dulce served them a belated comida, or main meal, and all the women began to plan their next move.

Even before they could think of a strategy, the old nurse gave them her news. Dulce, who did all the marketing here, had run into an old friend the day before. This friend, a Teresa, worked for a young couple who were renting a small house in the next section of Bahía, 'Marbella'. They were about to move to Riobamba, in the sierra, or highlands, and the friend would be out of a job.

Mara was excited to hear the news! She asked Dulce to go to the house right away, and see if it would be for rent again, and, if so, how soon. And, maybe, if she seemed suitable, the friend could stay on with the three from Paraiso!

So Dulce put on a large straw hat, and walking, went off to find her friend's house. The others began to straighten up the cottage, putting all the baby's things together with Julia's and Dulce's belongings. Mara and Benita simply put their packages and cases into the corner, not stopping to unpack.

It was only an hour and a half later when the nurse reappeared, removing her hat with a smile. "I found it!" she said. "The street is a short one, also on the beach, and everyone knew where Teresa lived! Doña Mara, I think you will like the little house! It's very clean, with only two bedrooms, however. But the kitchen comes with a stove!"

Mara was very pleased, but worried. The night of the flight with the newborn she had given Dulce all the money she possessed! Where was she to obtain enough for a monthly rent, food and clothing for the baby?! She immediately began to plan a stratagem to use on her husband, but had no idea if it would work!

"Well, as I said in the letter, Benita and I were to remain here for two weeks, and I mean to stay the whole time! Maybe, if I feel well enough, I'll even go into the ocean!" announced Mara.

"Aren't you well, mi Marita?!" Dulce looked worried.

"I'm just a little tired. I think I'll lie down for awhile. But let me know, right away, if there is any news from your friend." And she retired to the room Julia had fixed for her.

In a few hours, as the sun began to set in a glorious show of pinks and reds across the cobalt sea, Mara was awakened by Dulce.

"Wake up, Marita. We are saved!"

She sat up, only half awake, and sleepily listened to her old nurse as she gave her the news. The house was definitely for rent; the occupants were leaving in two days; Teresa would gladly stay on! And the cost, as far as her friend knew, was very affordable—only S50 sucres a month!

So the first week of her 'vacation' was spent in moving the little 'family' to their new home—a precious white wooden house facing the sea, and helping them make it comfortable and cozy for the two protectors and the baby boy who had been sent away from Paraiso.

Thirty-seven

Mara was determined to make her last week in Bahía one of relaxation. Her first goal was to explore the small city; the second, to tour the waterfront again.

Now that the little fugitive 'family' was settled in their new home, she had been able to send for the couple who had been given a 'vacation'. Jorge and his wife, Clara, returned, and, once again, cared for the house and its visitors.

Free from worries of household management, Mara took Benita with her to explore the town's amenities. They happily walked up and down the sandy streets and board sidewalks, popping in to see whatever beckoned from the shops' cluttered windows, roaming the seemingly endless, winding aisles of the outdoor markets.

Mara was grateful that the skirts for her new ensembles were shorter than last year, so that the hems were safer from whatever was strewn along the rather unkempt streets.

On the second day of their browsing about the town, Mara suddenly heard a familiar voice exclaiming,

"Mara!…I mean…er…Doña Mara!"

She looked out from under her parasol to see the rather red face of Captain Crowley. He looked, as usual, very distinguished in his stiff white uniform; handsome and smiling happily.

"This is a real surprise!" he exclaimed, speaking in perfectly pronounced Spanish.

"Hello, Captain! How nice to see you!"

"Perhaps we can get out of the sun?!" he suggested, as a crowd of young men almost pushed them down into the street.

PARAISO

"And have some tea near here?"

"Well," Mara began, hesitating. "Benita and I were…"

But the captain said easily, "Your maid could spend a little time on her own, I think. We could meet her in half an hour, right here."

Mara made a quick decision.

"Here, Benita," she said. "Take this cab fare and wait for me at home. Remember, it's #42 Vista del Mar."

They watched while she mounted a nearby cab, then walked together to a small coffee house.

Mara, unable to confide her real reason for being in Bahía, merely said that she was taking a short vacation and change of air. The captain, Joshua, could not get enough of looking at her. That hair! Those eyes! He had thought about them a great deal on his last two voyages. What a lucky man that Carlos Castañeda was!

The Englishman was a good person, and was sure this young girl was as innocent, unworldly and pure as she seemed. He would not try to seduce her, but he longed for her company.

"How is Paraiso?" he asked. "Is all going well as usual? The cacao business continues to thrive?"

He wanted to ask her if he could hold her hand, touch those full pink lips with his, but knew better.

"Oh, yes! Carlos takes such good care of the groves…and Eduardo too!"

"Will you be using your house here often?" he asked.

"Well, I don't know how often Carlos can get away. Maybe we can come again after the next big shipment goes out."

"I'm here so much," he remarked, "that I wish I had my own home, too, instead of staying at a hotel, or sleeping aboard."

Mara, a little confused by the actual conversation and the vibrations she felt behind it, was suddenly alert.

"You're looking for a house?!"

"Well, no, not actually 'looking'…just thinking it would solve a few problems."

"Oh…well…I had in mind…"she hesitated.

"Yes?" he prompted.

117

"Well, there's a very small house…occupied now by renters…that maybe you could buy…but the tenants would have to leave when you were here, of course…" and her voice trailed off. She had no idea *where* those three could 'go'!

He, realizing that this subject would prolong their relationship, decided to pursue it.

"Where is this house?"

And she described the beach-front home, and mentioned the possibility of a full-time maid/caretaker, wondering and worrying about the little 'family' in it.

They had finished two small cafés, and Mara began to feel uneasy about being seen alone with a 'stranger'! This was more than a mere passing in the street!

He also felt that he might have compromised her, and rose abruptly.

"Shall we go?" he asked, formal now. He lay a few bills on the table.

"Oh, yes, please." She rose, picked up her parasol and followed him out into the sun.

"I think I, too, had better be getting back. It's past time for the comida!"

He took her elbow and helped her into a cab, saying he would call at her house to let her know about the rental property.

She, inside the half-covered cab, felt a burning of her cheeks. She had never before been alone with a man who was not her husband or a relative, and felt that she had somehow dishonored Carlos!

What had she done? Why had she so easily accepted an invitation from a man almost a stranger, at least ten years older than she?! She was quite aware that 'society' would see this as both daring and foolish!

But, despite these sensible objections, she also knew, to her core, that she was a happier person now than she had been earlier this same day!

Thirty-eight

In only a few days Mara would have to leave this lazy, informal beach-life! She had passed hours walking barefoot in the sand and wading in the cool, foamy waves that slapped at the shore. She felt her real age here—a young girl, not a matron. She was mesmerized by the enormity and strength of the vast sea, stretching out forever to distant horizons, offering mysterious promises of an unknown future.

She was contemplating this watery vista one afternoon when Benita ran up to inform her that she had a caller, Captain Crowley. Not stopping to put on her shoes, she gathered up her long dress and walked back to the cottage through the sand. She sent Benita on ahead to say she was coming, so that she could rearrange her clothes and footwear.

But Joshua watched her from the small back porch, fascinated by the graceful picture he saw. There was no place to hide, so she mounted the steps, smiling, but embarrassed to be seen so informally.

"Buenas tardes, Capitán! Please excuse me, but I must have a moment alone. Just wait for me in the sala, please."

In just a few minutes she returned, now with the sand removed and shoes on. She asked Benita to see Clara about serving tea and cakes.

Once alone, she faced the young captain, who sat with a wrapped package on his lap.

"Well…welcome!…'What brings you here today? Did you have difficulty finding the house?"

"No, Doña Mara—none at all!…'But first, let me present you with a small token of my esteem…'and forgive me for not bringing flowers! None were fresh enough!"

And he passed her the gift.

While she untied the ribbon, he continued,

"Remember, I said I'd come if I decided about the rental house?"

She looked up from the package on her lap and replied,

"Of course. Would you like me to arrange for you to see it? When would you like to go?"

The tea came, with delicious little sweet cakes, and Mara filled the cups.

As soon as Benita left, Joshua smiled and continued,

"Any time that's convenient...May I call you just 'Mara'?"

"Oh, of course!" but first she opened the gift, and saw a small book called "*English-To Learn At Home.*" She couldn't read the title, but understood that it was a language book and opened it, going through the pages with interest.

"Thank you! I do love books, and studying! How kind of you to bring it!"

He, very pleased at her reaction, smiled happily.

"Oh, the house!" she exclaimed, remembering what she believed was his reason for the visit.

"Let me speak to my maid for a moment, please. Perhaps we can walk over right now."

So she rose, and left him alone with his tea, and conferred quietly with Benita in the hallway.

"Benita, hurry—see if they can all go for a walk! And try to hide the baby things!"

She returned to sit opposite Joshua, saying that they'd soon know if they could go over to inspect the property. Then the two sat quietly waiting, not saying much.

Joshua realized that this was dangerous ground! He should not have come! This young woman had bewitched him...and he felt powerless in her presence, wanting to say forbidden words, do dishonorable deeds!

Mara, unaware of the depth of his confusion, felt, though, a silent pressure in the air, so that she could hardly talk.

At last, Benita returned, and nodded to her mistress; they could go over to Marbella Street.

PARAISO

The three walked over to the little house, just a few minutes away. Mara tried to clear her head, breathe normally. Joshua, walking behind her and Benita, also took deep breaths, tried not to look at that golden head, that tiny waist.

It took only a few minutes' inspection to see that this was a decent little house, and, on hearing the price, he decided on the spot to purchase it!

Mara very carefully explored the possibility of the 'renters' staying on, at least until his return voyage. Yes, since these were his last three days before sailing to England, it would be ideal.

"If you don't object, Mara," (how he loved saying her name!), I'll write you when I'm sailing back...'to arrange for the house to be empty and waiting."

"Of course!" but Mara had no idea where the 'occupants' could go! "Do you know ahead of time, how long your stay will be? I'll have to inform the servants."

"Well, I'll let you know that, too."

In order to see her again, he invited her to come, with her maid, to inspect his ship the next day. She accepted happily, as this would give her a chance to see the fascinating wharves again.

So, with a formal handshake, the young captain departed, leaving a very confused Mara at her doorstep.

Now, if she could only persuade the captain to let the 'renters' be paid caretakers of his new property!...

The following day, she and Benita took a horse and buggy to the waterfront, where the captain was pacing up and down in front of his moored ship.

His face lit up when he saw them, and he escorted the two young ladies aboard. They were given a complete tour of the *Victoria*, including a climb down metal rungs into the engine room, not easily done in long skirts!

A young officer escorted Benita (at the captain's quiet order) to have lunch with those of lesser rank.

Mara sat with the captain at his private table, where they were served a special seafood meal, then left alone.

Joshua beamed with happiness, secretly thinking how wonderful it would be to turn pirate, lift anchor and sail away with this dream woman, never again to touch shore!

But she was more practical, and, after a rather stilted conversation on both sides, decided it was time for a lady to leave.

So she and her maid walked back down the gangplank and, not knowingly, left a poor man with a broken heart.

Thirty-nine

Not long after her return to Paraiso, Mara was able to confirm that she was, indeed, pregnant. So she attributed her unusual feelings in Bahía to this natural cause.

At the same time, Pilar confided to her that she, also, was expecting a baby.

Eduardo, determined not to be disappointed again, kept his enthusiasm at a very low level; happy, but cautiously so.

Carlos, though, was ecstatic! He loved his first two sons dearly, but this was Mara's child! He adored her to the point of veneration, and was determined that their child would have the world at its fingertips— girl or boy!

The two friends, Mara and Pilar, had the pleasure, during the next long months, of sharing their highest hopes, loving dreams and practical concerns. During the first phase of this time, the two spent long days 'next door' at 'San Rafael', also sharing Pilar's mother. María Otavia was a country woman, born and bred, and, as such, had the practical wisdom and abilities to be a real help to the two rather unskilled young women.

They spent hours together, sewing piles of coverlets, pillow cases, dainty shirts, sheets and diapers by the dozen. Later though, toward the end of the dry season, they were too clumsy to go even that short distance, so they stayed at Paraiso, learning from Dela how to prepare infant foods, and all sorts of other delicious recipes, better for their husbands then expectant mothers and babies.

One day, late in September, when the cacao harvest of August had been successfully packed and shipped, Carlos decided to ride to

Chone, alone, to see his banker friend and lawyer, César Nuñez, about Paraiso's earnings, and his will. He and Eduardo had decided that one of them had to be with the women at all times, even though the babies weren't expected until December; so he went alone.

As he rode through town, he was aware that a few of his acquaintances were quite cool in response to his greetings. When he had left his horse, Atena, at the stable, he walked to the bank, frowning with concern.

"César," he said to his friend, after shaking hands and settling himself in a comfortable chair.

"Has something happened here in town that I have not heard about? I take 'El Iris' two times weekly now, and I haven't read of anything unusual!"

César seemed embarrassed and, looking down, said,

"Well, there have been some ugly rumors floating around town! I first heard of them from the merchant from Bahía, the father of Cecilia Granados, you know: José Montenegro. He told me his son-in-law, Alberto, knew for a fact that your doctor, Fernando Cueva, had been murdered on Paraiso!"

Carlos half rose from his chair, an indignant look on his now-red face. He was speechless, as his friend continued.

"He is telling everyone who will listen that you and Eduardo must have had something to hide, and had to kill him to keep him quiet!"

At this, Carlos stood up and exploded!

"Why, that miserable tale-bearer! Whom does he think he's playing with?! If he's not in town, I'll ride over to Alberto's place and let him *feel* what a murder is!"

He was so angry that he could hardly speak, and his friend feared for his life. He was breathing heavily, his face beet-red, his jacket popping open.

"Carlos! Please! You're going to give yourself a heart attack!…'Slow down…I didn't say we, your friends, *believed* such nonsense! And José is not a bad man. Consider where he got his 'information'! Alberto Granados is the scoundrel here!"

Carlos sat back down and managed to breathe normally again. He

PARAISO

remained silent for a few moments, gathering his thoughts together, trying to imagine where this story could have come from.

Dr. Cueva had left Paraiso very soon after Pilar's baby had died; he had gone by river-boat with Clodoveo. At the time, both he and Eduardo were wrapped up in the events surrounding the newborn's death and burial. Why, he wondered now, hadn't the *doctor* delivered the child, not Dulce?! All the men had been left out, somehow! And where *was* the doctor now? He knew he had been alive and well until he stepped into that boat!

As suddenly as he had sat down, Carlos stood up again, saying,

"I, myself, would like the answer to the question of the doctor's whereabouts! And I mean to find out!"

He paused, looked his friend in the eye and said,

"César, that man was perfectly well until he left on that boat! There must be some witnesses somewhere who saw him leave that stormy night, or who saw him arrive here in Chone! And I'm going to find them!"

No matter how he concentrated, Carlos could not think of Clodoveo's surname, nor were he came from. He'd have to check with his overseer, Ernesto Cucalón. But, here in Chone, he could at least visit old Dr. Cueva, Fernando's father. He remembered that he lived in a stucco house on Mauro Ramos Idurarte Street, which he was sure he could recognize.

So he returned to the stable, had Atena saddled, and rode toward the place he remembered.

An old woman answered his knock at #55, and, with a worried look, said that the doctor was very ill, and could see no one.

"Go and give him my name, Señor Castañeda," ordered Carlos.

No one could argue with his tone of icy command, and her expression changed, a weak, toothless smile appearing amidst the wrinkles.

"Yes, sir...please step inside."

Leaving Atena tethered at a hitching post, he entered the dark hallway. He heard her footsteps, then silence. In a short time, she returned, and trembling, said weakly,

125

"I'm sorry, sir, but the doctor is very feverish, and sends his best wishes, but he is also in mourning and cannot see anyone!"

Carlos, angry and frustrated, wanted to shake the poor woman, but tried to control himself.

"Has the young Dr. Fernando been home lately?" he asked, his heart pounding.

The old servant's eyes flew open in surprise, and she answered, "No, sir. You see, he is dead!"

"Dead?!" Carlos repeated, now growing more worried still. "When was the funeral?! I heard of none!"

"We couldn't have one, sir. He couldn't be found!"

Carlos' heart was beating hard. Could it be that Fernando *had* been murdered?! He realized that to continue questioning the old woman would only add to the false story. So he turned to leave, saying,

"Please tell the doctor that this old friend, Señor Carlos Castañeda called and that he is very sorry for his loss, and hopes he will be better soon."

At this, he turned and left, leaving a perplexed old servant staring after him as he mounted Atena and rode away down the dusty street.

Forty

Carlos did not want to let another day, another hour go by without resolving this terrible problem! But it was already growing late when he arrived at Paraiso. He immediately found Pepín, and asked him to accompany him to the overseer's house.

When they knocked on the door, a large woman, wearing an apron, answered.

"Yes? Oh! Perdón Don Carlos! I didn't realize..."

"It's all right, Doña María; where is your husband?"

She, noting his unusual harsh tone, cringed a little, answering,

"Why, he is over at the 'La Cecilia'! but he only left after his work day!"

"Yes, of course," Carlos replied, in a sarcastic tone that was lost on the protective wife.

"Thank you," he finished, and turned and walked quickly away, followed by a silent Pepín.

When they were alone, Carlos said to his best worker,

"Pepín, please inform Don Eduardo that I'm going over to 'La Cecilia', and that you're accompanying me. I'll wait until you get Mercurio saddled."

Pepín was already sprinting toward the main house.

"Sí, Patron! I'll meet you near the Grove."

By the time the two men met at the entrance to the most important cacao grove, the sun was low on the horizon, but Carlos was determined to settle this urgent matter right away.

As they rode, Carlos gave Pepín a veiled account of the rumor being spread, with no names mentioned, only that the good doctor had come to an early end.

127

Pepín, as usual, was tight-lipped, but nodded as the information was revealed. He only said,

"I think we're headed in the right direction."

When they reached the neighboring plantation it was dusk, and the gardens and fields were empty. Already a few lights from oil lamps could be seen in several of the laborers' thatched huts.

At the door of the principal building, a simple wood-frame house with shuttered windows, Alberto Granados himself answered, in surprise.

"Don Carlos! What brings you here, and so late?"

"Be careful, Alberto," warned Carlos in an angry tone, "or I'll tell you! But first, where is your henchman, Cucalón?!"

Granados changed his neighborly attitude instantly.

" 'Your Cucalón'? Why should *your* overseer be here?" he asked, in his usual supercilious tone.

"Yes, why?!" replied Carlos in a soft voice.

Just as Granados was about to reply, a voice came from behind him.

"Who is it, Don Alberto? Any problem?"

It was Ernesto Cucalón, who, on seeing his tall employer filling the doorway as the sun's last pink beams glowed behind him, almost tripped and fell.

"Oh, Don Carlos! Ah, I was just leaving for home…just paying my respects to our good neighbor!"

"Come out here, you rogue! I want to see your face when I ask you about Clodoveo! Where is he, by the way?! You failed to report him missing, quite a while back! And where did our 'good neighbor' get his information about my boat, and Dr. Cueva in it?!"

At this point, Carlos was face to face with his employee, and was hard put not to strangle him. But he restrained himself, confronting Granados, instead.

"Where *is* our doctor?! What have you done with him?! I know he was here in that storm! If I don't get some answers tonight, your fates are going to be more than rumors!!"

It was dangerous talk, but Carlos, almost out of control with righteous anger, knew his limits, and he knew his 'victims'…both hypocritical cowards!

"I don't know what you're shouting about, and you're on *my* land, now. Take your crazy accusations and get off!"

No one had ever spoken to Carlos like that in his entire life, and all his inherent good breeding and clear thinking came to his rescue. He ignored this petty little upstart, and turned to his own most respected employee, Pepín.

"Pepín," he asked, "Have *you* heard anything about your co-worker lately?"

Pepín stepped up, his brown skin almost invisible in the growing dusk.

"Si, Jefe. Clodoveo was seen *here* after the storm. The doctor was with him, as they had to leave the sinking boat!"

"And how do you know *that*, you black Indian?! Where were *you*, sneaking around instead of working?!"

Pepín struggled to remain calm, true to his nature. He ignored the insult, and continued to speak to Carlos.

"Don Carlos, two of our workers have 'novias', girlfriends, here, and were stuck in the storm that night. *They* saw *our* Clodoveo *and* the doctor! And they also saw *our* Señor Cucalón!"

"Liar!" raged the overseer.

"No, Señor! I don't lie—*ever*! My friends saw that the doctor looked in a bad way, but they pushed the boat back into the river, with him in it!"

"Who is 'they'?!" demanded Carlos.

"This man," pointing to Cucalón, "and that," pointing at Granados. "They did it together!"

Carlos, unable to arrest the pair on the spot, and afraid he, himself would harm them, grabbed Pepín and walked away.

"Pepín, do you think you can get help in Chone tonight? Right now?…there's going to be a moon!"

"Of course, sir; I know just where the station is. I'll hurry!"

"Be careful, Pepín. You really know too much, but I dare not go. I don't have a weapon, so I can't hold these two murderers, but I *can* refuse to leave, and stand watch. I'll wait for you!"

Pepín ran to get his horse, and galloped off toward Chone, taking a shortcut through 'La Nelly', one of the smaller farms belonging to Paraiso.

Forty-one

It seemed that this dark night would never end! The two accused had taken refuge in the main house at 'La Cecilia', and their pacing silhouettes could be seen occasionally through the lightly-curtained windows.

Carlos, shivering now in the cooler night air, stood watch next to his warm horse, looking up, now and then, to gaze at the full moon and arching, star-filled black sky above.

He knew it was too soon to expect Pepín, but his hot anger had melted to anxiety. He wondered if all that had passed was simply gossip; if it had nothing to do with fact!

After an hour or so, he lifted his head, thinking he had heard a horse's hooves. He stood absolutely still, covering Atena's nostrils as she began to whinny. Yes, the sound grew louder.

Suddenly he heard a low call.

"Carlos! Are you here?" it was Eduardo!

"Sí, hermano. I'm over here," and he gave a low whistle to guide him.

Suddenly, Homero trotted up, and Eduardo slid down beside his brother.

"Carlos!" he whispered, as loud as he dared. "What's happening?! Why are you here outside?!"

"Sh, quiet, little brother! I'm waiting for Pepín. He's gone to fetch help in Chone."

" !Dios mío! What's happened?! I was so worried! I had to leave the women with Pablo."

"Well, 'our' Cucalón is in cahoots with this sorry 'neighbor', and we'll soon know why! They've done something with poor Fernando Cueva!"

"Oh, my God! Why?!"

"Sh, let's not talk any more! I want them to stay inside, where they are!"

Just then, they heard the sound of many hooves, and perhaps the wheels of a carriage.

And in a few seconds, several horsemen with lanterns, and a small vehicle came into the plantation's entrance yard.

"Don Carlos!" a voice called out, not cautiously.

"Sí, over here," answered Carlos.

Five men rode over to the two brothers, and another got down from the carriage, walking over to the group.

They were quite noisy, and, as they approached the house, the door was flung open, outlining the pair of suspects.

In the light that shone out from the entryway, the brothers could see that their uniformed rescuers were all armed!

"Stay where you are!" ordered their chief. "We're coming inside, so turn around and lead the way!"

When they reached the main sala, the two accused were trembling as they were encircled by their 'visitors'!

But Granados, always quick to play his habitual 'superior' role, taunted,

"You are all trespassing! This is *my* property, and you will leave immediately!" The chief officer, very relaxed and glad to be inside on this chilly night, merely chuckled, and said,

"Take it easy, Granados. Sit down, both of you!"

The other policemen were circled around the pair, guns handy,

Just then, after a brief knock, the door opened and Pepín came in, looking relieved to see his bosses all right. He stayed in the background while the chief interrogated Granados.

"Where is Dr. Cueva?!"

"How should I know?!" taunted the landowner.

"It is said that you and Cucalón, here, were the last to see him, the night of the big storm!...and...by the way, if you don't care to answer here, why, we'll just have to escort you to Chone!"

"I...we...know nothing about this matter! It is a problem of Paraiso's."

"How about you, Cucalón?!"

"Same here. why should I know?!"

"My, my; this is the last place several witnesses saw you two, and a certain Clodoveo..." at this, the chief turned to one of his men, saying,

"Pedro, take Oscar and go through the workers' houses. See if you can round up this guy, or anyone who was around during that storm!"

"Sí, mi jefe. Yes, Chief!" and the two left quickly.

"At dawn, we are searching the river for the boat, and a body, so be very careful what you leave out here! Any more to say?"

"No, of course not! Why are you treating us like criminals?!"

"Well, just in case, I'm leaving my deputy, Gonzalo, here, to keep you company tonight. You'll have to stay here, in the living room until you find something to say. He has a gun, by the way, and is very good at using it!'

At this point, Carlos stepped up to the chief and thanked him for coming, saying,

"I think we can leave matters in your capable hands, Chief, so my brother and I, along with my new overseer here, Pepín, will be going along back home to Paraiso."

"Yes, of course, Don Carlos. Buenas nochas to you, too, Don Eduardo; and thanks José...you're a good man!" he concluded, using Pepín's formal name.

So the weary men mounted their horses and headed back to Paraiso.

It was four-thirty in the morning!

Forty-two

By the time Mara and Pilar's babies were due to arrive, there had been many changes in their small world.

As the rains began, early in December, they no longer had neighbors living to the east at 'La Cecilia'. Alberto Granados was forced to save face by leaving his plantation, and taking his family to live in Bahía with his in-laws.

Though no crime had been proven, there had, at the very least, been negligence on his part, and he had been made to admit it publicly to the police and to the local newspapers, where the Castañeda name had been completely vindicated.

For poor Dr. Cueva had drowned that stormy night, and was already dead when the boat washed up on 'La Cecilia's' river bank. The 'crime' was that the two accused, Granados and Cucalón, had not rescued the body and delivered it for proper burial, but had thrown it back into the raging water, intending to continue the 'murder' rumor against the Castañedas, in order to discredit their neighbors and eventually take over Paraiso.

Pepín was now working as the overseer on Paraiso, while his predecessor, and co-conspirator in the case, Ernesto Cucalón, had also been forced to leave the vicinity, after serving only a month in Chone's jail.

Fernando Cueva's body had washed up again on the shore a week after these occurrences, and had been restored to his family. At last, his old father was able to give him a proper burial in the local churchyard, where he joined him a month later.

Clodoveo, the boatman in the case, had disappeared on that eventful night, and was never seen again in Manabí…

Pilar's baby was the first, and arrived on schedule, before Christmas; an adorable brunet boy, with his mother's ivory skin, pink checks and green eyes. Eduardo was so delighted that he was constantly in the way of the nanny, Alicia, wanting to 'help' with every phase of the infant's care. They named him after his two grandfathers, José Rafael.

Mara was fascinated with the newborn, as were the older boys, Eduardito and Jaimito, who hung around the cradle as often as permitted, checking to see if he was growing fast enough to be able to play with them soon.

On Christmas Eve, Mara began having contractions, and Carlos, so worried and solicitous, would not leave her side; holding her hands, wiping her brow, rubbing her back. Finally, 'Mama Chaco', the Uribe family's Indian midwife they had brought from Colombia, had to push him away, and finally, out of the room!

The baby boy was born punctually on the dot of midnight, and his mother radiated happiness. Carlos was by her side as soon as permitted, beside himself with love and adoration. Little Juan Carlos was a replica of his mother, from golden hair, big blue eyes and sweet smile that seemed imprinted prematurely on his face.

Now, the Paraiso family seemed complete and fulfilled. So many little boys to carry on the family's good name and reputation! It was a truly wonder-filled Christmas Season!

The next few years were blissfully happy ones at Paraiso. The babies were robust and healthy, profiting in every way from their mothers' growing skills.

The older boys were tall now, and handsome. Eleven and nine the year of the babies' births, the two attended daily classes in the old school-room/library. The tutor, Francisco Villalobos, now graying and more bent over than ever, patiently taught this new generation that held great promise, in his estimation.

****

Two years after Eduardo's son was born, came a lovely little daughter, also called María Pilar. The father doted on this little copy of himself; a sandy blonde with light blue eyes and fair skin. She responded from birth with happy gurgles, then outright laughter, and was a joy to her doting parents. Pilar's daughter, called only 'Larita', was the object of affection to all who knew her.

When Mara's little son, known from birth as 'Carlo', was two years old, the young mother developed a serious cold and a subsequent lingering cough. No local herbal remedies helped, and Carlos grew worried.

He was in the midst of clearing another portion of the jungle, preparing a new cacao grove, and was too busy to be home often.

Finally, he decided to send his wife to Bahía to see if the sea air would help her lungs. It was always beneficial, in any case, to leave this humid area at least once or twice a year.

So the plans went forward, and, after what seemed so many years, she was again packing, this time for two, for a trip to the shore.

Despite the heat, Carlos bundled his wife under several layers of capes and coverlets, lifted little Carlo up, and joined them for the trip to Chone, to put them on the next train for the coast.

Mara, coughing constantly, trying to keep her face away from her son, did not, this time, really enjoy the railroad trip. Luckily, Carlo slept much of the time, ate when given little snacks, and was generally good-natured, as was usual with him.

They were met at the Bahía station by their caretaker, Jorge Rivas, who loaded up their luggage into a rented carriage, and drove them to the cottage at #42 Vista del Mar.

The very sight of the glistening azure water spreading out from nearby, white-crested waves to the smooth horizon far beyond, lifted Mara's spirits as always, and she vowed to obey everyone's order for rest and medicines so that she could sooner return to her healthy self!

Clara, Jorge's trim little wife, fell immediately in love with the adorable child Mara brought with her. Who could resist those soft, golden curls, wide, sea-blue eyes and happy smiles?! And Carlo responded, accompanying his new-found friend everywhere throughout the days that followed.

When Mara first settled herself in the living room/sala, she noticed a white envelope lying on the table.

"It's for you, Ma'am," said Clara, noticing her mistress's glance and handing her the letter.

"It's been here for almost two months, Señora, and I have another one from last year."

Mara flushed slightly, remembering her somewhat secret order: not to forward any mail to Paraiso. With the unopened missile in hand, she looked up at Clara, and asked if Dulce had been by lately.

"No, Ma'am, not for more than a month. But I bumped into Miss Julia at the market last week, and she said her son is very well…now not so babyish, a big boy!"

"Oh," replied Mara, trying to hide her enthusiasm.

"I'm glad. I'll go visit them soon." And she let it go at that, knowing her constant, if small, financial help was keeping Luis a healthy, happy boy!

When finally left alone, Mara opened the letter, knowing it was from Captain Crowley. Sure enough, he formally sent her greetings, saying he was sorry to have missed her on his last trip, and announcing that he would be sailing for Ecuador again "soon", and hoped to be in Bahía at least by June, 1920.

Today was May 17, 1920.

Forty-three

Mara woke in the early morning, more than a week after her arrival in Bahía, suddenly feeling healed. As she lay in her bed in the hushed dawn-hour of the day, she could hear the waves rolling into the shore with a loud rumble, then, with a sucking sound, being pulled out again. The rhythm of the water's push and pull had been a lullaby the night before, and was now a daybreak's greeting.

She was alone, so as not to spread her cough to Carlo, and lay there letting layers of memories wash over her, like the waves outside.

Strangely, she did not think of her little adopted family here in Bahía, first. She felt a new heat in her cheeks, a blush, as she noticed the letter lying on the bedside table. She realized, as her eyes opened wide, that seeing Joshua Crowley again would be pleasant! Then sighing deeply, she felt that this was not a wifely thought, and should be put away somewhere, maybe on the shore, where the tide could pull it far out to sea, making it disappear forever. Yet, she was guiltily enjoying the thought, now, alone, where no one could see her face and read her mind.

She had been fast recuperating here in the beach-front cottage, and this morning was the first time she had awakened without coughing. It had already been arranged for her to see Dulce today, and she was determined to bathe, dress and stay up all day.

Just then, there was a low call outside the bedroom door.

"Mamá," called a soft voice.

"Yes, Carlito! Come in, darling."

The door flew open and her little son came toward her, a sunny smile on his face.

She hugged him, for the first time since leaving Paraiso, as she felt truly well now, but still gently pushed him back away from her, saying, "Good morning, precious boy! Don't get too close, yet. I'm almost well, but I can't kiss you for a few more days!"

Carlo was happy just to be near her, and did not mind that he was being taken right back out of the room.

"Stay in the hallway, darling. Maybe later you can sleep in here, after it's been cleaned and aired...anyway, I'm getting up today, and we're going to have company!"

After she was up and dressed, Mara went to the combined living-dining room, and Carlo, who had already eaten, happily played with this toys nearby, while she breakfasted.

As soon as the dishes had been cleared away, Clara announced that "Miss Mercedes" was at the door. Mercedes Morales had been 'Dulce' so long that Mara did not at once recognize the name; but soon they were face to face, and she enfolded the nurse in a loving embrace.

"Dulce! You look so well! How are you all at Marbella? And did you remember the instructions I gave you last year? You know, to pretend you were just visiting Teresa, in case the Captain showed up; and to come over here until he left?!"

Dulce, all smiles, returned the hug.

"You look your old self, Miss Mara! I'm glad to see you, at last! Are you well now?"

"I still feel a little shaky from being in bed, but I'm not coughing anymore! Where are Luis and Julia?"

"They're waiting for a visit from you. And, yes, we *did* remember to come over here last year; and a good thing we did! It was a complete surprise to see the Captain!...Wait 'til you see Luis...such a big boy now! Imagine, four years old!"

That very afternoon, Mara took Carlo to meet Luis and Julia. Mara was amazed and puzzled at the boys' resemblance to each other—her son and Pilar's! for both were sandy-haired and blue-eyed, and the two could be brothers to little Larita!

Still, Mara did not stop to analyze these observations, and was just happy that they could pass as siblings, and that they took to each other on sight! From then on, when they were together, they seemed to belong to a secret society, having knowledge of a mysterious password and language that no one else around could decipher!

The little house sparkled with order and cleanliness. The three refugees seemed so well settled in their daily routines that Mara was almost reluctant to move them once again. But if the Captain's latest letter was correct, they had only a few days to move back to the cottage, so that the Marbella house could be made ready for the rightful owner.

Mara, still feeling a little tired and weak, decided to spend money on a horse-drawn cab so that all their bundles of possessions could be moved at once, along with the little family. By nightfall they were again installed at #42 Vista del Mar, and the little white house was left empty, with only Teresa to care for it, until the English owner should arrive.

Jorge and Clara were delighted to have 'guests' and a house full of laughter and lively conversation.

Mara, a little worried about this uncommon secrecy, re-read the two letters Captain Crowley had sent. In the 'old' one, it was clear that he had expected to see Mara last year, and had been disappointed; and in the new one, that he would be in Bahía very shortly, surely by June, and hoped to see her again! He sent greetings to her husband and all the family at Paraiso.

That night, this time with Carlo next to her in a little crib, Mara lay in bed listening to the restless surf, pounding in, receding out, over and over, until, not daring to feel or think at all, she fell asleep.

Forty-four

Two days after moving Luis and his little 'family' to the cottage, Mara sat in her living room trying to make sense of her English book. The children were napping and the other women were all in the kitchen chattering while preparing the evening meal.

This language was really strange! It didn't seem related to anything she knew—Spanish or Latin!

Softly, she tried to pronounce 'table'; "taybul." Then, 'chair', "chare", 'pencil', "paynsul". She studied the vocabulary silently, then closed the book and tried to remember how to write the words. This was more successful, and after half an hour, she was able to spell them all.

Softly, again, she tried a 'conversation': 'Hello', 'How are you?', 'Fine, thank you'.

Just then, there was a knock on the door and Julia emerged from the now-quiet kitchen to answer it.

"Oh! !Capitán! Please enter."

Mara rose quickly, dropping the text book and blushing. She remained quiet while Joshua Crowley stepped inside, looking around the dimly lit room.

"Buenas tardes," he replied to Julia, handing her his cap, which she placed on a side table. Then, seeing Mara, he strode over towards her, as Julia left the room.

"¡Mara! Qué gusto! What a pleasure to see you!"

Mara, still a little pale from her illness, seemed very white to him, but with red cheeks.

"¡Capitán!" she said formally, "This is a pleasure for us."

Seeing a book on the floor, Joshua bent over and picked it up, glancing at the title.

"Oh, I see you are studying English!"

Mara blushed again, "I have just started...there really hasn't been much time...please sit down."

He sat on the little sofa, next to her, placing the book between them.

He drank in her picture there, like a thirsty man finding a lake in the desert.

"You are well?" he questioned with concern.

"Oh, yes," she managed to say, but her breathing had become irregular and difficult.

She seemed so fragile to him, too pale. But her golden hair framed her face like a halo, her eyes were deep pools that tempted a parched man.

Suddenly, his throat grew too dry to speak. He could only sit there, staring at her, a man seeing his dream come to life, and not believing his luck!

It was so quiet in the room that it seemed they had left it. The door to the kitchen suddenly opened, a protective Dulce peering around it.

"My little one, are you all right?!" she asked, her words coming into the hushed room like stones thrown into water!

Mara and Joshua were startled out of their silence, she replying, "Oh, yes, we're fine. Please bring some tea, Dulce."

The nurse, embarrassed to have been so abrupt, said softly,

"Yes, little one, at once," and backed up, closing the door behind her.

Mara rose, excusing herself, and began to light the lamps, brightening the room, which had become dim in the dusky light of early evening. Here, on the east side of the house, the ocean's roar could not be heard except as a distant sound; and at the end of the street as they were, all was quiet.

Sitting there together, they were aware of children's voices, then only low murmurs from beyond the doors.

"Mara, or should I say 'Señora'?! I have to ask you! Are you happy...truly happy?!" His Spanish was as good as ever, but she

PARAISO

detected a slight accent now, perhaps from disuse. And she was taken by surprise at such a blatantly personal question.

Now her cheeks reddened again.

"Yes, of course, I am very happy. I have my little son with me now!"

"Mara," he probed. "I think you understand me! These are our lives, our futures here on earth that I'm speaking of!" He was so earnest, so sincere, that he could not be ignored.

She looked up at him, sitting there so handsome and virile, his eyes probing hers, and she was forced to acknowledge his daring speech!

"Captain...Joshua...you know I cannot answer a question like that! I'm not free...on the contrary, there are more than a dozen hands holding my wings! I cannot fly, even if I wished it!" And tears came into her eyes, real water from those pools of blue.

"Oh, Mara! don't cry! I have to say it...I must! Can't you see that I love you...have loved you many years already?!" At this, he bowed his head, covering his face with his hands.

She was so moved at this voicing of his deepest feelings that it aroused in her all her hidden longings.

"Joshua...you shouldn't...don't waste yourself on me! I am so surrounded with love and obligation! I'm on an island here, and you need to roam the world and be free!"

He looked up then, restraining himself from taking her in his arms.

"But I will never be free! Don't you see that?! Everywhere I sail, I sail with you in my heart!"

"Oh, don't," she protested weakly. "You are wounding me with your words, hurting *my* heart!"

He was on the verge of breaking every social rule, ready to crush her to his chest, smother her with his needy kisses.

But the door opened once again, letting a shaft of strong light fall into the room. Dulce brought a tray toward them, saying,

"Here you are, Ma'am. Though it's a shame...tea so close to dinner!"

Mara and Joshua both jumped up, their nerves tingling with unsent messages.

143

"Oh! Thank you, Dulce, but the Captain has just told me that he won't be able to stay for dinner. He just dropped by to say hello, and now he's returning to his ship."

The broken man retrieved his cap, and, head bowed, said softly, "Don't do this Mara! don't send me away without hope! With one drop of 'esperanza' I can drink for as many years as it takes!"

She, unsteady on her feet, her soul joining his as her body stayed behind, could only gasp for air.

"I am your book, Joshua…you can read me…that has to be enough for now."

His heart leaped at this message of hope, and he went from the house into the darkening street with the sure knowledge that part of himself was in her soul.

Forty-five

Before Mara left Bahía the next day, she had a long, serious talk with Julia. The very pretty maid was now nineteen years old, a year younger than her mistress, and attracted attention wherever she went; for her swinging gait, long, flowing dark hair and beautiful face. Naturally, men were drawn to her, but because she went nearly everywhere with little Luis, they backed off a bit, thinking she must already be married.

All these factors served Mara's purpose, which was to retrieve Luis, and get him back into his true family. She pointed out to Julia that, though she had done them all a remarkable service, and had been completely loyal, she now should have her 'freedom'. (As Mara said this, she winced inwardly, thinking of Joshua's words the day before. *She* was not free!)

"Julia, in a year of so you won't be considered 'young' anymore. Most men like young brides, and you deserve to have your own life!"

Mara thought now that it was a good thing that they had agreed that Luis should not call her 'Mamá', but 'Julia', always. The little boy never asked about 'mother', but perhaps he wondered, and would certainly think about it as he matured.

"But who will care for him?!" asked Julia, tears in her eyes, for she genuinely loved the little boy.

"We'll see," said Mara. "I may take him back to Paraiso, but for now, Dulce can care for him"

Julia began to cry in earnest, sobbing out that she had no parents, herself, and no other family.

"Where will I go?"

Mara, her arm around the poor girl, answered warmly,

"Don't worry, Julia. *I* will always be in your debt, and will watch out for you! But I don't want you to return to the house on Marbella Street."

"I'm going to send you some money until you're employed. I don't have much of my own. Until you can find work, you can stay here and help Clara with the cottage...I think I know of a more permanent position, maybe in a store. Would you like that?"

Julia brightened at this, saying,

"Oh, yes, Miss Mara! I would like that much better than anything! And I can read a little, and also know my numbers, so that will help me, no?"

Mara smiled, "Yes, that will surely help. Now go and help Dulce pack up, and say goodbye to your little charge. He's going to miss you, and that's why I want to do this before he's any older!"

Julia had now stopped crying, and smiled at this sudden dream come true...to work in a store, and not do housework or baby-care day and night!

When she had left, Mara thought of her options. Dulce had heard that the English Merchant Ship in port was leaving today; that is, almost as soon as it had arrived! It seemed that cacao, always its main cargo, was scarce, and not selling well in Europe; and that there was very little to load.

As soon as she could verify this news, she knew she could use the Marbella house once more, if necessary.

Mara also knew that a widow-lady, formerly of Chone, had opened a dress shop here in Bahía, and she decided to visit her that very morning.

A little later, she was able to find the new establishment on Peru Street, and went in to speak to the Señora, Viuda de Urvina. When she told her that Julia was seeking employment, the lady clapped her hands happily.

"Oh, I *do* need help here! there is so much to do, and I, a poor widow, can't do it all alone! Please send her over today, and we'll see if she'll be suitable!"

Just for that, Mara immediately chose a new soft blue dress that hung gracefully to her ankles. The widow Urvina had a great selection of hand-sewn garments, and also filled custom orders. This was an ideal situation for Julia, so feminine and a gifted seamstress! Mara was very nervous now. She had planned to leave the town earlier, so as to be certain not to see Joshua again. Now, she must hurry and go!

Jorge, Clara's husband, suggested that she take the motor launch to Chone, via the river. It would be faster, and she could go to a neighboring plantation of Paraiso's, 'La Margarita', and then continue home by horse cart.

At the last minute, Mara made the decision to take both Dulce and Luis with them. The little boys were overjoyed at the news, and Dulce was happy to stay with them all!

Mara had heard by messenger that Julia had been hired at the dress shop, and could stay in the rooms above the store; so now the cottage was to be empty again, with only the caretakers to protect it.

Forty-six

While Mara was recuperating in Bahía, there were problems at Paraiso.

Carlos had not felt his usual vigorous self for many days now, and found it harder and harder to arise at dawn and work all day, as had been his custom all his life.

He could not understand what was happening to him, as he had always been so fit and strong. At first, he thought it must be due to missing his young wife, who always made him feel so virile. But, after waking with a slight headache one day, and feeling chilly on a very warm afternoon, he began to think it was something else.

But he ignored these incidents, and, not confiding in his brother, forced himself to go out to the new cacao grove every day, where they were transplanting carefully tended seedlings, not returning until night fall. At times, he would shiver in the filtered sunlight, or, become very warm, almost feverish. But he worked on stubbornly.

His excitement about the creation of the first new plantings in many years, thus adding some two-hundred new productive acres to Paraiso, made him return day after day to the beautiful, now-cleared virgin forest floor. The enormous canopy of giant jungle trees, a mixture of palo prieto, bucare and algarrobo, together with towering mangoes and higuerones, shaded and protected the baby growth below. In three to five years, the healthy new cacao trees would begin to produce their soon-discarded charelles, then the pollinated flowers and healthy pods, and would be ready to be pruned to a lower fifteen feet, for maximum bean production.

But, if they were to reach their goal of up to 1400 pounds of cacao beans per acre, much care would have to be taken, since, when the rainy season arrived in a few months, the tiny plants would have to be strong enough to repel the wet-soil attackers, 'Black Pod' and 'Swollen Shoot'.

For several days now, Carlos had been forced to sit down and rest for longer and longer periods. Pepín, his right-hand man, was able to keep the workers busy and productive, but was always aware of Don Carlos. He grew more worried as the days passed, and his employer seemed less and less able to stride along the planting beds as before, resting more and more frequently.

One afternoon, as the grove darkened with the setting of the sun, streaks of color flashed through the branches, as many birds winged their way up toward the light above, calling out to others as they flew. There, in the dusky light, Pepín found Carlos, head in hands, unable to stand. Alarmed, he sent one of the men back to the main house to advise Don Eduardo, and bring back a horse.

Eduardo arrived within the hour, and helped his brother mount Atena, leading him back home behind Horacio. Together with Pepín, Eduardo helped Carlos up the stairs to his room, where he fell into bed, shaking with chills.

"We need to get him to a doctor, or bring one here, but I'm not sure who that should be, now that the two Cuevases are gone!" Eduardo was frantic now, seeing that this was a serious matter.

Pepín, always ready to serve, offered to ride into Chone and inquire at their pharmacy for a 'good doctor'.

Eduardo, not wanting to leave his brother, agreed, and Pepín left immediately on his 'Mercurio'.

By this time, Carlos had stopped shivering and was bathed in perspiration, racked with fever, too dizzy to sit up.

Eduardo, more worried than he had ever been in his life, including at the onset of childbirth, sent word to Pilar that he was not coming for their evening meal, but would sit with Carlos, at least until a doctor came!

The whole household, hearing of the master's illness, fell quiet, and everyone went about his or her duties as silently as possible.

Before Pepín returned, Eduardo heard a horse and cart in the drive, then at their doorway. Mara! what good luck!

Eduardo rushed down to receive her, and break the news about her husband before she heard garbled versions from the household help.

He was amazed to see *two* little boys, *and* Dulce, climb down after Mara, all disheveled and very tired from their trip. But there was no time for inquiries.

Mara looked for her husband, but Eduardo immediately drew her aside, saying softly,

"He's very ill, Marita. We've sent for a doctor, who should be here soon."

Mara, hearing this, felt faint. She was already exhausted, not only physically, from the responsibilities of their trip, keeping two active boys safe on a small boat, but mentally, after all the planning and resolving of secret problems.

She went upstairs immediately, leaving Dulce to care for the boys, and, after a cenita, or supper, to put them to bed in Carlo's room.

On seeing Carlos, now shivering with chills again, she felt a deep anxiety, and a stab of self-blame. For *she*, in spite of *her* illness and the various solutions she had had to come to for answers to delicate issues, *she* had been on a vacation of sorts. And, she thought guiltily, a man had declared a secret love for her!...to a married woman...in her husband's house! What a scandal that would be, if known!

To see her husband helpless in their bed brought tears to her eyes, and she embraced his cold, shaking body with love, as well as remorse!

Carlos suddenly writhed in pain, and began to retch, then fell back on the pillows. For a while he lay quiet, sweat beading on his forehead. Mara felt helpless, as she applied damp towels to his face. She could not take in that this was her powerful, masterful husband, the guiding compass of her life! For half an hour he seemed to sleep, and she sat as near to him as possible, clinging to his hand, softly stroking his arm.

Pepín arrived at the entrance door, still dirty from the grove and looking more disheveled than ever.

A few minutes later, Eduardo entered the room, a wild look in his eyes.

"I don't know what to do!" he confessed, speaking in a low tone. "Pepín says the pharmacist was sure he had a bad form of malaria! And that no doctor in Chone is trained to treat the disease like a Dr. Martínez in Bahía. Mara, we have to take him there as soon as it's light tomorrow! You will have to go with him as I *can't* leave, with all our other problems!"

Mara stared at him, so tired mentally and physically. How was she to make that trip again in just a few hours?!

"*What* other problems, Eduardo?! What has happened since I left?!"

Eduardo pulled her over to a far corner of the room and said in a low voice,

"I haven't even told Carlos, yet! But, for the first time, I have had to borrow heavily from the banks! There is a lower demand for our beans in Europe right now, and we simply can't survive without this help!" he was frantic with worry, for his brother, for their future!

Mara sighed deeply, trying to pull herself together. Here in this room were the two most important men in her life; and each, in his own way, was asking, begging for her help!

She touched Eduardo's sleeve, saying,

"You can count on me. Just stay with him a few hours while I clean up and rest. Then I'll leave early in the morning! Please have Pilar watch over the boys; Luis, Carlo's little friend, is visiting us, so please treat him well!"

With that, she bent to softly kiss Carlos' damp forehead, and left to sleep in the guest room.

151

Forty-seven

Pilar sat quietly regarding Carlo and the 'new' boy amusing her son, a puzzled look on her face. Would Mara play this awful prank on her?! Her stomach ached and she felt dizzy.

"Pilar, my darling, what's wrong?"

Eduardo was preparing to leave for his office, where he planned to spend an hour or so before going over to supervise the work at the new grove. A deep frown creased his forehead. He was a worried man, and his wife seemed to be suffering from his problems. He should have hidden his concerns better!

Pilar just shook her head and continued to stare at something her husband could not see. She sat with her mending half done in her lap, the sewing basket on the edge of a footstool. Suddenly, it toppled over, spilling the contents everywhere.

And Pilar, who normally would simply have bent to retrieve her threads, scissors and pins, didn't move or even seem to notice. Eduardo, feeling selfish at having concentrated solely on his own problems lately studied his wife closely, then leaned down to pick up the rolling spools and pins, dropping them all into her basket.

As he straightened up, he noticed a few more buttons on the floor, and threw them in with the rest. But suddenly he stood there, frowning, a puzzled look on his face.

"Pilar!" he reached back into her basket, picking up a familiar-looking button.

She looked up then, and the children also stopped playing, watching their elders curiously.

"Isn't this the button Carlos has been missing for years now?!"

"I'm not sure," stammered Pilar, not able to look at her husband.

PARAISO

"Mamá," called Rafito, as José Rafael was called.
"Don't cry, Mamá!" for tears had welled up in Pilar's eyes.
"Dulce!" she called out, and the old nurse appeared at the door.
"Please take the children outside now. Thank you!"
Eduardo watched them leave, then turned back to his young wife,
all his love in his look mixed with puzzlement.
"Why did you never return this to Carlos?" he asked.
At this, she bent her head, and the memory of finding that button
became too much to bear. She began to sob at the recollection, and
because she had deceived her husband about so much!
"Pilar, my love! Don't cry! What is it…this puny little button?! Tell
me, right now; what's bothering you?!!"
He lifted her up from the chair and led her to a small sofa in the
room, his arms enfolding her.
"My dearest! Speak to me! You know you can tell me
anything…that I will always love you, no matter what you say!"
At this, Pilar turned in his arms and buried her face on his strong,
familiar chest. How she loved this gentle man; how she longed to bare
her innermost secrets to him! Still, she hesitated. Perhaps he would no
longer love her, knowing all that she had done to preserve the little
perfect picture of their marriage. She knew with certainty that she
could not tell him a *part*, only, of the truth; *all* would have to be
revealed!
"Oh, Eduardo, my sweetheart, best love—my life! I have a terrible
secret to tell you!"
He, a forty-year-old man, looked down at her shiny black hair, her
lovely Madonna-like face feeling the wealthiest man alive! How could
she, such a young woman still, at twenty, have such a heartbreaking
'secret'?! Surely she exaggerated!
But Pilar, growing braver in the circle of his loving arms, plunged
ahead.
"Eduardo, I have sinned, and been sinned against, but I confessed,
long ago, and was forgiven by the Church!"
Now he sat up straight, loosening his hold, amazed and aghast at
this announcement.

153

"What?! *What* sin? Who sinned against you!??"

"Before we were married," began Pilar, also sitting up, wiping her eyes on his handkerchief.

"Someone violated me, and I became pregnant!"

Eduardo, dumbfounded, could not move. He felt that a bullet had entered his heart.

"You? Violated?" he could hardly speak.

"Who would do this?! *Before* our marriage? Then…when you were expecting so soon…that was *not* my child?!! He could not believe what he was imagining!

"No, dearest," she said softly. "It was the violator's…and that's why…"

"You killed his child?!" Eduardo interrupted. "How *could* you kill an innocent baby?!" and he stared at Pilar, seeing a different woman.

"No, no, no, my husband! How could you think that of me?! No one was killed! On the contrary, he was saved!"

"Saved??" Eduardo was totally confused and growing angrier by the second. He stood up, confronting her.

"Didn't the baby die?! I saw him…there was nothing wrong with him! How could he suddenly die?! That should have been God's choice…not yours!"

At this accusation, Pilar began to sob again, and now Eduardo looked at her in disbelief and anger.

"What are you trying to tell me then?!" he demanded. "*What* are you 'confessing' to me?!"

She looked up at him imploringly.

"Eduardo, listen to the truth! I'm so sorry never to have told you! I should have trusted you; instead, I trusted priests and servants!!"

Totally puzzled, he sank back down beside her. It was impossible for him to remain angry with this trusted woman who held his life in her palm. She was his everything, no matter what had happened or would happen in their future together!

"My darling, listen…" and she bowed her head, remembering that fatal afternoon at the river. Then, she started there, telling him all, up to the 'burial' of the baby boy.

154

Eduardo was stunned, his eyes wide, first with incredulity, then understanding. He had been brought to the conclusion, but had to ask. "Then...the button? Where did it come from? Why is it here?!" But he felt the truth before he heard it.

"I...found it...on the river bank...I don't know why I kept it...I didn't want to forget who had hurt me...us!"

Eduardo stood up again, a deep sadness in his eyes, and a mounting anger.

"I'll kill him...my own brother!" And he began to weep.

"No, darling...you are no killer, either. Let us go on pretending...so Mara will never know!"

Then he turned to this angel God had sent him.

"But if the baby's not dead...where *is* he? Where has he been?"

Pilar looked up at him with eyes full of love and pity."

"He's right here, my dearest. I think he's Luis!"

Forty-eight

The last twenty-four hours had seemed like a lifetime to Eduardo. He had so much new information to absorb, and with it had seemed to have gained a 'son', and lost a brother.

Pilar, at last happy and at peace with the past few years, and tranquil at having her son safe and here, under their very roof, now slept a deep and refreshing sleep in their 'new' bedroom in the main house.

But Eduardo was unable to close his eyes after the shocking news of the river incident, and the knowledge that 'his' dead son was here, alive *and* was his brother's child, with *his* wife!

It was too much to sort out all at once! His mood swung from an anger so red-hot and deep that murder seemed the only solution…to a profound sadness that had touched his perfect marriage!

He wept at times, choking on his tears, at Pilar's sullied innocence at this betrayal by his own brother…a brother who had been his idol and best example of manhood all of his life!

At last, with the coming of dawn, his active mind, so fraught with problems and possible solutions, grew weary; his body became limp where he sat on the chaise longue in their bedroom, and he fell into an uneasy sleep.

But not even an hour had passed when the morning bell sounded, reverberating through the compound around the main house, and over the out-buildings, groves and fields beyond.

As he sat up, dazed and weary from worry and lack of sleep, he heard a loud thudding knock on the entrance door below, accompanied by calls of his name.

He was still dressed as he had been the evening before, but his jaws sported a new stubble, and his hair fell over his forehead.

"What is it, my love?" asked Pilar in alarm, as she sat up, still half asleep.

"I don't know, mi amor. Go back to sleep. I'll be back in a moment."

He thought guiltily that it might be news of Carlos—bad news—and he went to answer the door, disheveled as he was.

When he had pulled back the bolt and the door swung open, there was Pepín, repeating his entreaty.

"Don Eduardo! Please accompany me to the main grove! I fear we will have a really poor season!"

"Stop a moment, Pepín! What exactly has happened?"

"I don't rightly know, Don Eduardo, but there is something strange about the plants! I rose early today, and walked over to the home grove...things look different...very different!"

"Come in, Pepín. Go to the kitchen for some coffee while I dress. I'll be back in ten minutes!"

Pepín looked confused, as he saw his 'jefe' dressed already, but went back toward the kitchen as Eduardo raced upstairs.

Pilar had not gone back to sleep, and was waiting for him in the hallway.

Speaking softly so as not to wake the children, she asked, "What is it, darling? I am so worried! And you look so tired!"

He gazed at her with all his love in his eyes and soft smile.

"Don't be upset, my angel! I just need to see what's happening in the grove. Pepín didn't explain the problem too well."

They entered their bedroom and, as he spoke, he began to tear off yesterday's clothes and grope for fresh ones. At the vanity table, he paused to splash water on his face and run a comb through his hair, though he took no time to shave.

With a quick, but satisfying kiss on his young wife's lips, he dashed out of the room and down the stairs.

Pepín was waiting for him, hat in hand, and they went out together.

Instead of trying to get more information from his favorite employee, Eduardo just strode as quickly as possible towards the nearest grove.

Entering it had always been an almost religious experience for him.

To leave the 'outside' world and enter into this darkened retreat, under the taller, stately guardians that hung over the delightful lower canopy of dark green shade that the cacao trees provided, was so like entering the hush of a church or cathedral.

Today, though, the hush seemed more menacing than soothing! He stopped and squinted against the darker expanse, trying to decide what was different. For there was a difference.

Growth was always accompanied by a feeling of uplifting exuberance, but today there was a funereal air to the atmosphere, almost of death!

Pepín looked at his master's face, trying to read an explanation, as Eduardo looked downward at the floor of the grove. And he gasped inadvertently.

There, blossoming in the soft, leaf-covered undergrowth, were myriads of tiny rose-pink toadstools, innocent in their babyhood-deadly in their message!

He quickly examined the new shoots on the branches, and the pods growing on the trunk. Both men slapped at unseen insects biting their necks and wrists. The workers wore only neckerchiefs and straw hats, but the owners never entered this place without their pith helmets, high collars and long sleeves, which Eduardo had not stopped to do today.

He felt a wrench deep in his gut, as if he had received a strong blow in boxing. What was he to do against this almost invisible enemy! At this moment, how he needed his brother—*his* new enemy!

He knew full well that there was no 'cure' for this known, well-documented foe. There was no magic 'spray'—no way to stop this tropical plague known as 'Witches Broom'!

But he said, as calmly as he could,

"Pepín, get at least twenty men, or more, over here right away. Bring tools to clean out these toadstools, but don't leave them on the ground! Pile them into spread-cloths, and burn them outside as fast as you can!"

"The pods and new shoots seem all right for the moment, but we have to hurry!"

And they both went out to face the rising hot sun with heavy hearts.

Forty-nine

Since arriving in Bahía, Carlos seemed to be better, but it was difficult for him to walk, so he lay all day on a comfortable chaise in the main sala, where Mara was with him constantly. But it frightened her to see this vigorous man laid so low, with hardly enough energy to sit up or eat.

Jorge, their cottage caretaker, had found Dr. Martínez, and had brought him to see his employer as soon as he and Mara had arrived. The doctor was a man of about sixty, who radiated knowledge and confidence. He was of medium height, and a little swarthy. His intelligent face was accented with heavy brows and a small goatee, and was completed, so to speak, by a pair of pince-nez eyeglasses on his prominent nose.

He had examined his new patient thoroughly. Then, with a grave expression, he took Mara aside, speaking in a low voice.

"Naturally, Ma'am, I shall have to do some work in my laboratory first, but I definitely believe that your husband has a form of malaria— a very serious form. I have written prescriptions for medicines to be given at once. But we'll have to wait for his next attack to be more certain. Send for me at once if the fever or chills come back!"

With these instructions given, he donned his high hat, bowed slightly and wished Mara a "good day."

So Mara had sent for the prescribed quinine immediately, and Carlos seemed to respond favorably; being able to sleep all night in his bed, and having no symptoms for several days.

On his second visit, the doctor had sat down privately with Mara, whom he had come to respect for the excellent care she was giving Carlos.

159

"Señora, you asked me how your husband could have been infected after living so many years without any problems of this sort. For some reason, your plantation now has infected female anopheline mosquitos, who may have been carried there from far away. One would have to inspect many properties to be sure. There is only one thing to do on *your* plantation, and that is to try to eradicate any of these insects—mainly by treating their water and breeding grounds."

"But, Señora, I am sorry to say, your husband's case is not the usual kind seen here. He, I believe, has the most serious type, cerebral malaria. I don't like to worry you, but I *must* prepare you. I found 'plasmodium alciparum' parasites, which will affect his blood, and even his liver, kidneys and lungs; and he may go into a coma. We have to give him the medicine intravenously immediately!"

Mara was stunned at this terrible diagnosis, and felt her life slipping away from her! The doctor needed her assistance, though, so she helped him as he gave Carlos his medicine through his veins.

But when he had left, saying he'd return the next day, she felt faint, and sat down, her head whirling. Was she about to lose her dearest companion, her love and guide!? This man had been her teacher, and had tenderly shown her that every day was a gift, no matter where you lived; that there was something to learn from the trees, grasses, birds and every living creature under the sky. He was a man of Nature, robust and hearty; he had put all that he was into Paraiso, and it had responded with abundance.

And now, Nature seemed to be on the Evil side of life, wounding this hardy man with the tiniest of enemies!

A few days before, Mara had sent the worker who had accompanied them to Bahía, Pablo, back to Paraiso, so that Eduardo and Pilar could know how Carlos was. But she was not expecting such a rapid response!

Instead of a letter, there was a loud knocking on the Cottage door at about six, two mornings later; and when Clara went to answer, there was Eduardo.

Mara was shocked at his appearance. Instead of the well-groomed, handsome brother-in-law she was accustomed to seeing daily, this man was red-eyed and unshaven, his hair hanging over his forehead. His clothes, too, were wrinkled and did not appear to have been changed lately!

"Eduardo! What is the matter? You look so tired!" Mara said tactfully.

"I must see Carlos at once!" he responded, after embracing his sister-in-law.

"Let me see if he is awake. He's very ill, Eduardo."

Eduardo flinched, his eyes filling with tears.

"I know," he said softly. "I know. That's why I must speak with him."

Mara was able to get Eduardo to sit down, and asked Clara to bring hot coffee and rolls. Then she went to see her husband, who had heard noises and was wide awake.

She kissed him tenderly, telling him of his brother's arrival. He seemed so fragile that she did not even consider moving him to the sala. Instead, she fluffed his pillows and helped him sit up a little, arranging his pajamas neatly, and combing his hair.

"I'll bring you some juice and coffee, darling. Is it all right if Eduardo comes in now?"

He nodded weakly, so she left him to get his brother.

Eduardo was shocked to see his mentor, once such a powerful leader, laid so low. He saw that Carlos had lost much weight, and instead of his usual ruddy complexion, had a pallid face and now-faded blue-gray eyes.

"My God, brother! What has this done to you!?" And he bowed his head with a sob.

Carlos reached for his hand, saying,

"It's only a malaria attack, hermanito. I'll be all right as soon as the medicine starts to work!"

But Eduardo was not reassured! This was not the malaria he knew. He hesitated, not wanting to alarm this sick man; but he knew that Carlos was the only one who could help him and all of Paraiso.

"Carlos...hermano...something terrible has come to Paraiso! I think we have 'Witches' Broom'!"

161

Those last words fell like a boulder on Carlos' consciousness. Witches' Broom! Nothing inspired more fear in the hearts of cacao plantation owners! And he knew that Eduardo, for all his knowledge, could not conquer this alone. In fact, probably no one could win over this tropical evil!

Then, Eduardo told him what they had done, so far, and Carlos concurred with his actions.

"But you must go to *all* the groves! All the affected branches must be cut off and destroyed by fire. The new plants are probably worthless now; so if there are toadstools there, you must burn all those plants!"

Here, he sighed deeply, resting, not able to speak for a few minutes, but his adrenaline gave him the strength to go on.

Carlos half-sat up.

"Brother, it's very important not to let those tiny flowers blow into the air! That's how they got there, maybe from many, many kilometers away. Read my notes, in my journals, you know where. It's 'crinipellis perniciosa', a fungus, and it comes from tiny spores on those pretty toadstools!"

He leaned back down into his pillows, exhausted from talking so much. There was a soft knock on the door, and Mara entered with a small tray, her husband's breakfast arranged neatly on it.

She made a sign to Eduardo, and he rose to leave the room,

"I'll be back to say goodbye," he choked out.

"I must leave for Paraiso right away!"

Before he left, Mara gave him some of Carlos' clothes to change into and he washed and shaved. He emerged from the room looking refreshed, and more like his old self again.

But he had a haunted look in his eyes that Mara had never seen there before. She believed it came from his brother's illness, and Witches' Broom, never dreaming that Pilar was concerned!

After a quick, but hearty breakfast, Eduardo went to his brother's room to say goodbye.

As he embraced him, he said softly,

"I forgive you, brother!"

Fifty

Eduardo's mood matched the beginning of the rainy season: he was irritable and nervous as the skies began to let loose torrents of steamy water, drenching the soil and dampening the spirits of all who lived and worked on Paraiso.

Since his hurried return to the hacienda from Bahía, the problems with the new cacao plants and older trees persisted, growing daily more severe.

Each day, the workers had faithfully hacked away at the affected branches and pods, burning tall piles at every grove. As Carlos had predicted, the new plantings were a total loss, shriveling up from 'Black Pod' and 'Swollen Shoot'.

The former, 'Black Pod', was caused by phytophtora, a fungus, which spread rapidly on the pods, affected by these unremitting torrents of rain, and insufficient sunshine, in lower temperatures than usual. It was too late, now, to use the sprays of copper salts that were required, though they were doing every other known thing to combat it.

'Swollen Shoot' was rampant. This virus, which could be stopped temporarily, mutated to other forms that eventually made the plants fatally vulnerable.

Now, the orchards were being attacked by these plagues plus a virulent form of 'Witches' Broom', or crinipellis perniciosa, a fungus causing wilting cherelles (or new pods), 'cushiongalls' and 'diebad'. These spores turned tender cacao shoots into hardened, leafless and fruitless branches, hence, *the witches' brooms*.

All these diseases were a combination of physiological, viral, nutritional and fungal conditions, and were leading to the destruction of more than twenty years of planning, executing and harvesting on one of the most successful farms ever to exist in Ecuador.

Eduardo was sick with worry about the destruction of a lifetime's hard work, and about his very ill brother. He tried to rally the spirits of the workers, along with the faithful Pepín; and he tried to stay calm and strong with Pilar and all the family, who now were totally dependent on him!

How he missed his virile, active brother! Somehow, he felt that the diseased plants were his fault, and that Paraiso would be safe and healthy with Carlos' return.

But now he was alone, not realizing, through lack of good general communication, that all of Manabí and Guayas provinces were suffering the same fate! The spores of infection had traveled miles each night, spreading disaster in their wake. This once-stable 'Grano de Oro', or 'golden grain', a world-renowned staple for the making of chocolate abroad, was to be wiped out, as they had experienced it in their generation.

And still the rains persisted unrelentingly, falling without pause, day after dreary day, with not a sign of sunshine in more than a month! Nature was fast becoming the enemy instead of the usual cheery, cooperative, life-generating spirit that it had been.

As one sodden day after another passed, the laborers resorted to working barefoot, as their shoes and sandals were ruined by the mud.

There came a day when there was literally nothing more they could do! It was all but impossible even to enter the sloshy groves, and all had been done except to actually cut down the older trees!

Pepín García, as overseer for the main plantation, was able to ride into Chone one time, only, to confer with the bankers that Eduardo had dealt with for loans. However, he came back discouraged and empty-handed, as the banks had refused to extend more credit. This was a region-wide problem, and the story was similar even in the neighboring countries. Peru and Brazil were having lesser, but similar experiences.

Now, for the first time in the existence of Paraiso, Eduardo was unable to pay the workers. He opened the store to them, not charging for needed, rationed food and goods. So the men stayed on in their free housing, living precariously on their meager rations.

But the day came when first one family, then another, bundled their possessions into back-packs, and walked off the hacienda, never to return! This fact was incomprehensible to Eduardo, who had loved his companion-workers, and had treated them as 'family' all his working life! Many came to say their goodbyes, but others went sheepishly off into the night.

The house servants were the last to desert the family, and several stayed, faithful, sharing their employers' fate. Dulce, now growing old, but still an energetic helper, was among these; as were Dela, the cook, and her daughter, Zenaida, as well as Benita.

'Mama Chaco', the old midwife, had passed away the year before, and both Rosa Mendoza, the housekeeper, and the maid Alicia, had returned home to Chone.

Francisco Villalobos, the tutor, was forced to leave this home of more than two decades, and had gone to Portoviejo to be teacher to the three children of Felipe and Elena Palacios. Father Juan Bautista had left to join his brethren in the Jesuit monastery in Quito.

Now, the little 'family' that was left on this 'island', deserted and 'floating' on the sodden earth, trembled as they faced their fate!

Eduardo knew that he had no options left. There had been no shipping out of the treasured beans for months, and no incoming revenue! There was a little left of the large loan from the banks, for Eduardo was an excellent and thrifty manager.

But nothing prepared the remaining occupants of Paraiso for the lone rider who cantered down the main road from the west early one morning, splattering rocks and mud in his wake.

This 'visitor' was a solemn young man representing the main bank in Portoviejo, where most of their banking had originated. Señor Alejandro Enríquez stayed but half an hour—enough time to refresh himself, drink hot coffee with 'chifles', or fried green plantains, and empanadas, and deliver this doom-filled message:

Paraiso was now the property of the banks, and the family was required to vacate immediately, leaving all household possessions and furnishings behind!

Fifty-one

Now there could no longer be any procrastination or hesitation. The feared 'hour' had arrived! The remaining family must prepare to leave their beloved home—their Paradise!

Eduardo had no other man in this crisis to help him with all his decisions. Only Pepín and a handful of workers remained on the 'empty' plantation. And now that there was no pursuing of physical outdoor activity, it remained only to sort the office papers and household goods for an orderly withdrawal.

Pilar, a strong and loyal young woman, would not let her husband bear the burden alone. She organized the domestic routine so that she could leave the children most of the day, joining Eduardo in his office. She was the logical one to help him organize his ledgers and files for removal, as she was not only literate, but was quick at figures.

Together, they chose the most important documents, and Pepín carried duplicate records and other unwanted papers outdoors to burn.

The two married lovers, though deeply saddened, were comforted by being together, apart form the family, where they could embrace and share kisses, in spite of their desperate situation.

Ten days after the eviction warning, all was ready for departure.

Even though they had dismantled the cribs and beds to take in the wagon, along with their numerous suitcases and boxes, the furniture so dearly bought and preserved by the family since the last century, had to be left behind.

Even had they desired it, there was not one neighbor left with whom to leave their most precious pieces; so the cherished piano sat deserted, along with all the chairs, couches, rugs and chandeliers in the large sala. They brought with them what would fit: silverware, a few candlesticks, lamps and some kitchen utensils; but most possessions stayed behind.

Eduardo and Pepín finished closing all the shutters, nailing them down where possible. The key to the grand front door was turned, and Eduardo, tears in his eyes, left the only home he had ever known, and joined his little family, smaller now since the two older sons of Carlos, Eduardo and Jaime, had already left two days before, to live with their uncle, Alonzo Palacios, and his wife, Susana Aguilar, on the banana plantation belonging to her family. Dela, too, had also left, going back home to Chone with her daughter, Zenaida.

So he helped Pilar, the four children, Dulce and Benita mount the wagon, then joined them, his horse tied behind.

He had already embraced Pepín, to whom he had given fifty acres, still 'free' of the bank's claim, along with the deed, and left him to guard as he could the empty house.

It was still raining, so the plan was to get to Chone, then continue by railroad, horse and all, to Bahía.

But even as they were leaving, the first of many of the hungry and discontented workers began to close in on the now-deserted hacienda; and the first of the windows was broken, and the first pieces of Castañeda family history were taken.

****

When the remaining family arrived in Bahía, where the weather was brisk with salty breezes, they had no idea that they were symptomatic of this epoch in their country's history. A depression lay over the land, indeed over the whole of the Western world; food prices were high, exports in general were down, the Ecuadorian sucre had little value, and there was widespread discontent, especially among the working class.

In the 'next door' province of Guayaquil, where the country's largest shipping harbor employed thousands, workers' riots were so severe that bloody massacres had occurred. These events, followed by similar ones in the Andean highlands, helped the cause of the trade unions that were formed, and also brought about a chain reaction in the central government—but did little more than replace one clique with another.

Eduardo, standing alone, as it were, in the midst of this terrible personal and country-wide depression, felt, initially, unequal to the Herculean task of saving everyone, from Carlos and his loved ones, to his own little family.

But Pilar only became stronger in the 'storm'! She made Eduardo feel the most loved man alive, the most capable, the most judicious, which he was! She simply made him use what Nature had given him! Together they wrestled with the torrent of problems thrust upon them, and brought peace and harmony to the family.

After deciding with Mara where they should all fit into the now-bursting cottage, and arranging the rooms and their possessions, they held a family conference, but without Mara. Carlos was so ill, he was isolated from them all, and not consulted. But *he* was Mara's first concern, and, not wanting to leave him, left everything in Eduardo's and Pilar's hands.

They had brought food with them…all salvageable fresh fruits and vegetables, and many provisions left in the plantation store. Now, the highest priority was for Eduardo to seek employment. His oldest child, José Rafael, was ready for school, as were Luis and Carlo. They decided that all three should attend a Catholic day school, 'La Immaculada', but it was not free. The first of their meagre savings would go there.

The two women, fast friends always, had already spoken of working, also. Julia now ran the Viuda Urvina's dress shop, and was saving to buy it one day. She asked Pilar and Mara to sew or knit items to sell, for all three to share any profits.

Eduardo paid a visit to a local bank, not affiliated with the Portoviejo one that had taken over Paraiso, and they assured him that a position would undoubtedly open up soon; to call on them again the following week. He was highly recommended, they said, by their friend in Chone, César Nuñez.

There was nothing more they could do at the moment. But now Eduardo was forced to think about his brother.

Fifty-two

Carlos, lying in bed in the rear room facing the sea, heard many new voices and the shouts of children. With his eyes closed, he was sure he could feel his life force draining from his body.

That life ran through his head…from his carefree boyhood on a benevolent Paradise, with his best friend and brother. Their childhood had been so innocent—so clean—away from city problems…just the two, roaming the farmlands, exploring the jungle…climbing the impossibly tall trees, swimming in the river…studying together…always learning, from their father…then the tutor…taught to think deeply…to solve problems…to lead and to build.

Their quiet, loving mother had been a refuge from punishment meted out for infractions of a set of exacting rules. She was their haven in times of pain or grief; when a pet died, or when their knees bled from high falls. And she had made all their clothes herself, even with many servants around her, just as she baked delicacies for her sons and husband.

And Mariana (he thought of her then) had been so like her—so patient and willing—so devoted to living her life in the shadows, so that her Sun could shine!

…His Mara…so different—not of the shadows—but of the full sun! She was the warmth of his mature years—bringing laughter and understanding to his daily life. How he had loved the girl—and now this blossoming woman, who had given him every gift a man could ask for! Her very voice was like medicine to him now. And when she sat by his bedside, where she remained most of every day, he felt a relaxing of his body's turmoil, bringing him a daily peace.

Was Death to be like this—a remembering and then a forgetting—for eternity? Or, would he wait for his loved ones in some shadowy place, so that they could all travel together toward the Light? He wanted the answer, and struggled to think about it, but he was tired—so tired.

He could hear a knock, but didn't open his eyes. Dr. Martínez was speaking softly with Mara—too softly to understand.

"I am so very sorry, Señora Mara, but now there are all the signs of an overwhelming nature: your husband's liver and kidneys are not functioning normally, and he has the acute symptoms of respiratory failure, as well."

"I'm forced to admit defeat, as it appears that the small blood vessels of the brain have been invaded, too, and are blocked...In short, my dear lady, Don Carlos is, even as we speak, sinking into a coma..."

"Quickly, Señora, bid him goodbye! He may not hear you in an hour!"

Mara, horrified at this sudden and extreme worsening of events, embraced Carlos, putting her mouth near his ear.

He heard her, the last words he understood, as she whispered, "Carlos, my darling, I will always have you in my heart!"
****

By the time Eduardo was told of his brother's relapse, it was too late to say goodbye.

One by one, the family entered the sick room, where Carlos lay, breathing but unconscious. All said their farewells, leaning down to his still form.

Eduardo, in a shocked state, embraced the man who had been his life's companion and mentor, tears flowing over his anguished face. He had not said his 'adios' to a conscious brother, and now it was too late!

Pilar stood by him, her face deeply saddened at her beloved husband's bereavement, but still unable to kiss the man who had brought her so much pain.

Then, she thought of little Luis, a ray of happiness in their household. He stood there, with José Rafael, not knowing exactly who this still man was. But Pilar suddenly felt a greatness growing in her, and gave Luis her hand, saying,

"Kiss your father goodbye, darling," and Luis obeyed.

Eduardo stared at her in amazement—at her courage and goodness! This angel had come to save them all! He embraced her, folding the two little boys into their arms.

Carlo clung to Mara, trying to be courageous, but feeling bewildered by all the grownups were saying and doing. But finally, he, too, led by his weeping mother, went to the bedside and kissed his father.

"Goodbye, Papá! I shall take care of Mamá for you!"

Fifty-three

Alberto Granados, true to his widely-known nickname of 'El Grandioso', or 'The Great One', was secretly relieved when his father-in-law suddenly died, making him, through his wife, Cecilia, a rich man.

He had bitterly endured the general scornful reaction to his public confession of complicity in the Dr. Cueva-Castañeda scandal. But his necessary retreat to the soft life of his wife's merchant-family in Bahía had served, not to make him grateful for such a soft cushion to land on, but to sharpen his envy and feelings of hatred toward Carlos and Eduardo Castañeda and all their family.

Now, not having an interest in, nor talent for running the mercantile 'empire' his father-in-law had left for them, he turned to his wife, Cecilia, to take over the physical property, leaving him free to satisfy his driving need for revenge.

The young mother was to be the sole parent of their four children, managing the store and all it entailed of foreign orders and commitments, while her husband managed to get all the actual cash she'd inherited, and went off to Chone to deal with his erstwhile 'enemies'.

There, he bought back his own 'La Cecilia,' and also the adjoining properties of the Castañedas, including the jewel of 'El Paraiso'.

The bankers were delighted to get 'real' money for their condemned and confiscated, and now worthless properties, while Granados celebrated by moving into the hated family's main house.

He found this his first disappointment: it had been vandalized and emptied of everything possible of removal.

However, he brought a dozen or so servants, happy to be employed again, even though poorly paid, who cleaned and scrubbed until the empty house sparkled. Only the piano, too heavy to move far, and one or two other pieces of large furniture remained. Every chair and table had disappeared! The windows, too, on the ground floor, had all been smashed, and had to be replaced. The first of Alberto's 'cash' was beginning to disappear into the pit of endless repairs.

He brought in men to cut back the now-encroaching jungle, to repair the drying racks and rails, and to clean out the dying cacao trees. He had heard what he considered 'tall tales' of 'Witches Broom', and he started to harvest any remaining healthy pods.

He had similar crews working over on his former hacienda, 'La Cecilia', as well as on the eight surrounding, former Castañeda properties, but he preferred to eat and sleep at Paraiso.

It took only a few short months to spend most of 'his' inheritance and it became increasingly necessary to take in a big harvest in order to continue.

But the 'good' cacao pods were few, and the damaged ones plentiful, and the 'Great White Planter' was soon forced to recognize the truth!

Witches' Broom was here, and getting worse, since no measures were taken against it.

Finally, a hangdog Granados was forced to go into Chone and face the bankers once more.

"Señores, please be reasonable! Give me more time to right a badly run plantation! And we'll soon have a bumper crop!"

"Meantime, though, I do need a little loan to get me through this season, so I can get a shipment out…"

The bankers, César Nuñez among them, listened, though with barely controlled expressions of condolence.

"This is too bad, Alberto, but we can't give loans to non-producing haciendas! When you've sent out your first big shipment of beans, let us know, and we'll talk!"

All the men present were friends of the Castañedas, who had hated to see the most creative, innovative and productive farmers of their entire nation go down so ignominiously; and to see this untalented and vengeful man trying to replace them was offensive to their cultivated and sensitive natures.

There was nothing left to do but put a good face on this 'slap' from these new enemies, so Granados rose stiffly and huffed out of the building.

Knowing it was useless to return to the haciendas, he decided, after a few cooling drinks at the bar of his hotel, to catch the next train back to Bahía, and his erstwhile-deserted family.

What he was to say to his once-pretty, now overweight and 'aging' young wife, he had no idea. But the trip served to give him time for reflection and inventiveness. So that, on reaching Bahía, he was ready with a story made to melt an enemy's heart.

But, unbeknownst to him, his wife was now one of the latter, an enemy! And a clever one!

She had heard what he was up to at Chone and the plantations, and was seething at the loss of all the money her father had saved for forty years; of its having been stolen by a man she now loathed!

So, she, in turn, mortgaged part of her store's worth in order to buy more goods from Europe. Her father had taught her well as a young girl, and she knew exactly what and where to buy in order to make a good profit.

Any day now, she expected a new shipment; and the minute she made a significant profit, she planned to pay off the bank, and start saving any excess, until she could once again have a positive cash flow.

Her eldest child, son Adalberto, was now thirteen years old, and Fernando was eleven; their two sisters were Elena, nine and little Elisa, five. The girls were still too young to help, but both boys had small tasks in the store, and seemed to enjoy the work. They liked talking to customers, stocking the shelves and sometimes entering money into the cash register.

Cecilia knew that there was no chance for a divorce in this Catholic marriage, but, in her heart, and sometimes even on her lips, were new vows: never again to accept Alberto into her arms! She would do what she could, with the aid of a lawyer friend of the family, and others, even to keep him out of their home! This was daring for the day and place, but Cecilia had been an only child and much-loved daughter, and wanted to honor her father by using her head in this matter!

She had heard about Carlos' death and the present state of the Castañeda family, and greatly sympathized with them! She knew all too well what it meant to be in an unhappy situation!

So, when she met Mara or Pilar on the streets, she went out of her way to be cordial and pleasant; and this courtesy was never to be forgotten...

When Alberto Granados arrived back in Bahía, without his tail between his legs, and full of bravado, he was met by an entirely cool family.

In fact, Cecilia had packed up all his belongings and sent them south, down the coast, to a relative's in the port-town of Manta; and it was there she hoped he would follow! However, Alberto stayed a month or so to fight for what he claimed as his: first, the business, and second, his family.

But, not welcome in his wife's house, and unable to continue in a hotel, he angrily, and with many threats and forewarnings, was forced to follow his clothes!

Fifty-four

The sea was rippling in a slight breeze: white-frosted wavelets, sparkling, reflecting the July sunshine, far out to the horizon.

Mara stood on shore, letting the sand sift through her bare toes, watching this perpetual movement of cobalt and cerulean, feeling warmth and an unidentified restlessness…yearning and a practicality pulling her out, splashing back in, endlessly, hopelessly.

"Mara! Look!" Pilar came up to her, pointing out a dot on the farthest line that touched the sky. Slowly it grew, until, five minutes later it became a ship; and, in twenty, was a merchant vessel, flying the British flag.

Unconsciously, Mara became breathless and rigid, not moving, not daring to hope. Was this then the 'sign' she had waited for all her life?!

Pilar watched, alternating between the boat and her dearest friend. She could almost guess what she was thinking and feeling.

Right after Carlos had died, another English ship had come, bringing the orders from the many Manabí businesses, but not with its usual crew. Joshua Crowley had not been its captain, but the new one had brought a letter for Mara.

It was a formal note, but with an undercurrent of disguised messages, saying that he had been transferred temporarily to the Caribbean, but hoped to be in Ecuador in two years, at the most. He "prayed" that Mara (the "Señora") would be there and "would remember him". He would come calling to the house. He sorely missed his "friends" in Bahía! He ended with "the most sincere and heartfelt wishes" for their good health.

Mara had read this letter often, and wondered if she would really see Joshua again. She, herself, during the first agonizing months after Carlos' death, had tried hard not to think of anyone except in the immediate family.

She and Pilar had gone regularly to the Widow Urvina's shop to leave their knitted and sewn garments. These had sold so well, Julia always asked for more.

Eduardo had a well-paying job at the bank, where he was now the head accountant, as well as the chief loan officer.

The three little boys were thriving at school, and Pilar began to teach sunny Larita at home.

It was a peaceful little household, full of the laughter of children, and the love of two devoted mothers, doting father-uncle, and gentle servant-friends.

****

Without the rest of the household being aware, Mara went to her room immediately after seeing the ship. There, she washed and arranged her hair. Then, she tried on three dresses before deciding on a filmy white one, decorated with blue flowers. She was anxious and calm by turns; feeling the same pull of the tides, out and in: wonderful and depressing by turns.

Pilar, thinking she was resting, did not disturb her for afternoon tea, not knowing that Mara, wide awake, stood by the window, studying the gulls swooping down on the bright water, thinking of foreign ships and foreign ports.

A knock on the front door broke the afternoon quiet, and Pilar opened to an older, but handsome Joshua Crowley.

He was all smiles, asking for the 'family', and distributing little gifts among the children, and boxes of chocolates for the adults.

He looked around, praying to see Mara, but she was not there. His heart plummeted, thinking all kinds of disastrous thoughts.

Just when his automatic smiles began to waver in unhappiness, the door from the hallway opened, and Mara stood there like a vision!

He was so grateful that he wanted to fall on his knees in thanks!

Instead, he leaped up from his chair and went to meet her, taking her hand and bending to kiss it.

"Señora," he began, looking self-consciously around at Pilar. But she was smiling softly, with downcast eyes, so he turned back to Mara.

"Mara!" all his heart and soul was in that one salutation.

She knew it, felt it, and reciprocated, but said only,

"Capitán. Joshua, how nice to see you in Ecuador at last!"

Feeling claustrophobic, he begged,

"May we walk a little outside?"

Mara glanced quickly at Pilar, who rose and nodded.

"Go ahead; it's too warm in here! Excuse me, but I have to feed Larita." And she smiled and left the room.

Mara, blushing, nodded, and the two left the house. But they did not walk on the street. Instead, Joshua, taking Mara's arm, led her to the beach.

He had so much to say, was bursting with it, but could hardly breathe, feeling only her soft skin, and stood paralyzed.

She glanced up at him, feeling his very blood sending her messages through their hands.

"Two years! I thought I could never walk here again! How I have missed you, Mara!"

In fact, he had been true to his heart; never once, in all the ports, had he been with a woman, or indeed, *any* company. Instead, he had stayed mostly aboard his ship, pacing the decks, while his crew rambunctiously went ashore.

He had written hundreds of forbidden and unsent love words to Mara. And now, at last, he wanted to deliver them all in a real embrace, kissing her each message!

Mara, knowing in her woman's heart of his hunger, silently put pressure on his arm, turning them back in the opposite direction from her house's view. When they had walked in the sand for five minutes in silence, hand in hand, she faced him, not wanting him to suffer one second more!

"Tell me this is true-real-Joshua! It's like a dream I often have that's never finished!"

His blood boiling, he put his arms tightly around her, pulling her close to his chest.

"Mara, Mara, kiss me, my darling," and he bent his head down so that their lips could meet.

All her fantasies of romance seemed to hold her there, where she felt safe and wanted like never before. This was her knight; and she, a willing princess.

Their kiss seemed to last for hours, uniting their souls, and neither wanted to part. But he, knowing he could not go on without danger, pulled back, saying,

"Marita, darling. Marry me at once! Come with me to England! Stay with me forever! Will you?! Will you?!"

And she, gasping from the spiritual and physical effects of those deep kisses, gasped,

"You know I will, you know I have to! Just don't leave me again!"

Fifty-five

Mara became Mrs. Joshua Crowley before her twenty-third birthday. They were wed in the presence of the small family, only, in a tiny neighborhood church. The priest, a Father Julio, knowing there was no time to give lengthy instructions in the Faith to this likeable foreigner, taught him as quickly as possible so that the pair could have a true Catholic wedding before their ship was to sail.

This took place two weeks after Joshua's arrival. Meantime, beside his religious studies, he had been busy arranging their return trip on his ship, *King George V*. He had given orders to have the extra adjoining cabin to his made ready for his bride and son, moving his willing Chief Officer, or 'Mate', to another smaller one.

For they were to take Carlo, five years old, with them, separating him from his dearly loved 'cousin', Luis, seven. Both little boys were unhappy at this severing of strong ties, but both were brave.

The prospect of going on a huge vessel, with Mamá and a new Papá, who was the most important man on it, wearing an imposing white 'Masters' uniform, with much gold braid, kept a little boy happy, despite his loss of family.

And Luis, with a strong character and optimistic nature, was willing to part, as long as they would exchange letters, promising never to forget each other.

Joshua, who had been shocked to see the Castañedas' fortunes sink so low, wanted to help those staying in Ecuador. Of them all, he knew best how the whole Western world was suffering from an all-inclusive depression, and knew that a small country like theirs, with an undiversified economy, was more vulnerable than most.

He had no fortune, but offered his little house for whomever needed it, and the family was very grateful. For *their* cottage was bursting with so many, and Eduardo thought that young Eduardo and Jaime, Mariana and Carlos' sons, could now live there, with a tutor and an all-around servant, until they were older. He knew that Alfonso, good and generous as he had been, was now hard-put to keep them, since he and Susana had started a family of their own.

At the same time, Eduardo was so liked and respected at his bank, that they had offered him a loan, with easy repayment, so that he could add onto the cottage. This he was planning to start almost immediately, changing the house into a two-storey one, with more bedrooms and other amenities...

The whole family, servants included, went to the dock to say their farewells to Mara, Joshua and Carlo. Joshua had secretly ordered a tiny sailor suit to be made in town, and Carlo proudly stood on deck all in white, waving a new British flag.

Pilar cried so hard, leaning on Eduardo, that she could hardly see the ship pull away from its moorings, its horns sounding mournfully. All the little family cried openly, too, watching a waving Mara become smaller and smaller, as the big ship glided out to sea.

On board, Mara was discovering the delights of living at sea.

True, she had wept as she saw her little family disappear from view, and the shoreline of her adopted country blur into a dark line, then vanish.

But having Joshua's strong arms encircling her at the rail, with her little son at her side, she knew that this fresh start was right for them.

Joshua gently led his new little family inside, and to his cabin. He had only been married three hours, but he knew, too, that this was the way life was meant to be. He had waited thirty-three years to have the woman he had always dreamed of; had loved now so many years already!

He settled them in his comfortable quarters and gave orders for a luncheon to be served them there. Then, kissing Mara tenderly, he excused himself to go to the Bridge once more, saying she and Carlo could rest after eating, and that he'd return as soon as the ship was well on her way to Buenaventura in Colombia: their next and last stop before going through the Panama Canal.

After eating, Mara put Carlo down for a nap in the smaller, connecting cabin, while she, too excited to sleep right away, looked around her new surroundings.

All was so ship-shape, everything neat and in its proper place: almost invisible in the many built-in cupboards, drawers and shelves. She went to a wire-screened book shelf, and glanced over the titles. Her new husband obviously liked to read, and had a small collection of the classics mixed in with nautical stories and modern poetry. She was surprised to see Jack London represented, (a North American author she had heard of, but not read), and opened a book of his short stories, to 'Planchette'. The illustration showing a man and a young woman intrigued her, but the words were impossible for her to translate. What was 'voice', or 'pleading' or 'fallen'?! She scanned the page and recognized a similarity to Spanish in 'determination' and 'desperately', but it was all too complicated. So she leafed through the pages, enjoying the drawings, before finally returning the book to its shelf.

Then, suddenly feeling a relaxation of all the tensions of the last few days, after such a rush of planning for her wedding and this voyage, she lay down and closed her eyes.

So when Joshua returned a little later, he found both mother and son fast asleep. Smiling, he covered his new wife with a light blanket, then left again to guide his ship north up the western side of South America, on its last lap before turning east toward the Caribbean.
****

When night came—Mara's first at sea—she was entranced by the starlit sky over the black water, and surprised at the cold breeze blowing, in spite of their following a tropical shore.

Joshua held Carlo up to see the moon, and look down at the trailing white foam behind them.

Then, they all went to the cabin, and Carlo was put to bed.

For the first time since their vows, the newlyweds were alone; both trembling with happiness and anticipation.

It had been more than two years since Mara had stood in privacy with a man—her husband. And in spite of having been completely natural and unselfconscious with Carlos, she now felt suddenly shy and inadequate for this new, all-engulfing love. He was everything to her, and she wanted to be the same for him.

He, never having been married, felt he was being rewarded far beyond his merits, and longed to be enough for this exceptional young woman!

They stood there in the soft lamp-light, feeling the roll of the ship purring along in the calm waters, waiting to close the gap of a few inches.

She reached for his hand, pulling him close, and he stepped forward to engulf her in his arms; and all the tension disappeared.

Gently, he helped her remove layers of clothing, then lifted her onto his wide berth. His own uniform lay in disarray on the cabin floor, and he joined her, at last his own; and possessing her seemed a gift for his years of waiting, that he still did not deserve.

Mara felt fulfilled as she had never been; a completeness, two as one, that was so much more than merely physical; a uniting of two searching souls, who had found each other at last.

When, after a long time, they felt sated, they slept truly together, rocking on the gentle sea.

Fifty-six

The big merchant vessel flying the British flag steamed ahead, approaching Colón and the Panama Canal from the east. It was just past dawn, the sun already up behind them, the officers on deck alert and checking their advance with binoculars.

Carlo, wearing the uniform and insignia of Third Officer (or Third Mate) stood on the Bridge with his father and the Second Mate, whose adjutant he was. The two checked the charts and protocol instructions for passage through the locks.

They would be boarded in about half an hour by a pilot, and later, Measurers, who would inspect their manifests and other ship's documents for toll-collection purposes.

Carlo had gone through Cadet training while still in school, and, besides his voyages 'home' to Ecuador, had made two shorter trips with his father's ship. At eighteen, school finished, he had been promoted to Third Mate and was making his first long journey as an officer: with his father as Captain, and his mother as passenger.

He was now over six feet tall, and looked much as had Carlos Castañeda at the same age: a handsome sandy-haired, blue-eyed and muscular young man.

But he could also have been his English father's 'real' son: for Joshua had very similar coloring and build. And, he had been a true father to 'Charles', the only one Carlo clearly remembered.

The two men were, besides, good friends, and Carlo's disposition very much resembled Joshua's kind, gentle nature.

The little family of three had made two other similar trips together,

184

visiting Ecuador when Carlo was nine years old, and again in 1932, when he was fourteen.

Mara, now fluent in English, with a charming Latin accent, spoke almost always in Spanish with her son. And, if Joshua was present, he, too, practiced his wife's native language with them. Carlo had proved an excellent scholar, and excelled especially in languages and the arts. As a day-student in a local prep-school, he was a natural leader and peace-maker. But something in his soul called him, and he was restless, searching for something unidentifiable. Somehow, these infrequent sea journeys seemed to be the key to his finding the mysterious answer.

****

Mara knew better, as a veteran of thirteen years' acquaintance with the Merchant Navy, than to communicate with her sailor men during a maneuver such as the present one. So she stood peacefully at the rail of the *George V*, watching and enjoying the familiar scenes of the Canal once again, with its neat rows of army houses, set in their evergreen squares of lawn, palm trees waving down every street.

The sailors also knew better than to make their only female passenger uneasy by any untoward behavior; but they still enjoyed seeing the Captain's beautiful wife: admiring her golden looks and kind manner.

Far from being an Albatross to them, she was a good luck omen far from home!

Carlo, too, was enjoying the special thrill of the Canal: such a miracle of engineering ingenuity! In spite of the concentration necessary in the next fifteen hours it would take, start to finish, to cross the isthmus, his poetic nature saw beyond the locks, channels and 'cuts' to the wonder of the lowland tropical forests. His heart sang at the return to a Nature that seemed to be his from birth: the bright greens, mysterious lagoons, with their groves of cativo, korey and mangrove trees, accented with the endless variety of colorful plumage of hundreds of darting birds.

As usual, the wait in Colón, in line for authorization to proceed, in tandem with one other ship, took almost seven hours. This prelude would be followed by the now-familiar trip through a short, sea-level section here, and at the western side; then, three pairs of locks, the elevated section of Gatun and Miraflores Lakes, and then through the continental divide in the Gaillard Cut. At the other side, they'd go down through the Pedro Miguel locks, and back to deep water: fifty-one miles in total!

By the time the *George V* was on the Pacific side, in the bay of Panama, the crew was relieved from their extra duty, and the next shift took over.

Mara and Joshua were finally able to have a private meal in his cabin, and retire together.

Carlo, though, ate with the crew and shared a cabin with another junior officer, so his parents wouldn't see him until they were well on their way south, down the west coast of Colombia.

Fifty-seven

Mara stood at the railing of the *George V* as her husband guided the heavy ship into the port of Bahía de Caráquez. She glanced up towards the Bridge, and felt a thrill of pride to see, also, her handsome son, working alongside her captain.

She felt such a rush of emotion as she turned toward the shore of her beloved Ecuador! How she had missed its gentle people—her family! She tried to identify the Cottage, though she knew it had been modified once more, but the whole seafront, for kilometers up the coast, seemed to have houses where there had been only open land before.

Now they were close enough to see crowds of people waving from the pier; and soon she could see Pilar and Larita with Eduardo, and several young men and women she couldn't identify.

As soon as permitted, Mara came down the gangplank to embrace her family. Carlo, also, came down to greet them, shaking hands all around, giving Luis a giant hug. He, too, was as tall as his cousin, a good-looking man of twenty, with his now-darkening light-brown hair, blue-gray eyes and flashing grin. They quickly agreed to meet later, and Carlo dashed back up to his duties.

Joshua waved from the Bridge railing, but stayed there, smiling down at 'his' family. He, too, was feeling the pull of the simpler life of this bountiful, unspoiled land.

****

The first thing Eduardo wanted was to show Mara the 'new

house'! With all the family trailing behind, they took a taxi to #42 Vista del Mar. Mara had seen changes in the 'Cottage' in 1927 and 1932, on their previous visits, but the little house of her honeymoon with Carlos had now *totally* disappeared.

On the same site was a completely renovated and imposing building. Now a modern home altogether, it still had the charm of years gone by, with its wide veranda that almost entirely circled the building. All the bedrooms, up and down, had access to porches with sea views, and protective rolling shades of bamboo. Now, there was even a third story, with a viewing tower, complete with binoculars, a large study and more bedrooms.

A modern kitchen and various bathrooms boasted all the latest fixtures from abroad.

Mara especially liked the sala, which was both pretty and comfortable, with soft-cushioned tropical furniture, native plants and wide window views.

Gone were the oil lamps of her youth, replaced with modern lighting and ceiling fans whirring above.

Was she really thirty-six years old?! Pilar, too! She felt youthful still, and Pilar, was, if possible, more beautiful now than ever! Both women were wearing stylish clothing of the day—softly draped prints ending at mid-calf; and both still drew admiring glances wherever they went…

Larita was now seventeen, and was as pretty and cheerful as she had been as a small child. Her light blue eyes twinkled with mischief, still; her smile was an invitation to laugh. She still attended a convent day-school for girls, but her brother brought home his many friends from the 'Eloy Alfaro' high school, and José Rafael (or 'Rafa'') was never quite sure which friendships were his, and which were his sister's!

There was so much catching up to do with this growing family! So much had happened since 1932!

The 'big boys', Mariana and Carlos' sons, Eduardo and Jaime, were now young men of twenty-seven and twenty-five.

Eduardo senior, their uncle and head of the family, was fifty-six years old, and the president of his bank, besides being an elected officer in the state assembly of Manabí.

Both nephews had worked with him as bankers; but though 'young' Eduardo had stayed on with his uncle, Jaime yearned to get back to the land, and was working with Alfonso on the banana plantation. The two brothers had lived in Joshua's house for years, but now it was empty again, except for Teresa, the aging maid (her friend, Dulce, though, had died two years before).

Felipe was still in Portoviejo, and also managed a branch of his bank. He was happily married there, and he and Elena had four children.

Luis, who was ecstatic at having Carlo back, was the intellectual of the family…already, at twenty, writing articles for the local and national newspapers, and corresponding with a few of the outstanding men of letters in the widely-known 'Grupo de Guayaquil'.

All his contemporaries had grown up believing that he was Eduardo's son, as well as Pilar's. For the parents, this was true, and no one doubted that he was theirs! He was loved as their 'oldest', so much like Eduardo in spirit that it seemed 'obvious' to family and strangers alike. With their devotion, he had grown up to have faith in himself, developing a strong, happy personality.

And, like his father, he had, from childhood, grown to love poetry; so that, by this time, he had filled many notebooks with his words. Some of these appeared in newspapers occasionally, but only with the initials E.L.C.

****

Carlo could hardly wait to finish his duties so that he could join his family, also! Foreseeing this, Joshua had planned ahead, and everyone still in Bahía was invited to a formal dinner that evening, on board the *George V*.

Just at dusk, a long line of fashionably dressed men and women boarded the huge, still-loaded ship, and heard strains of native music being played on deck by a popular group from their city.

Joshua and Eduardo, kindred spirits, sat happily surveying the group, both admiring and toasting their lovely wives.

"Don Joshua, you are a perfect gentleman, and an Ecuadorian by nature! Come, bring Mara back and live here in Bahía!"

After a little wine, Joshua was all too happy to confide in this noble man.

"I haven't told Mara yet, but I plan to retire in two years. I'll be forty-eight, and will receive a good pension from the company! She's been in England for thirteen years now, and has never felt warm!"

Both men laughed and drank another toast to their beautiful women and all their children and relatives.

Mara, glowing with happiness, spoke to Pilar about all sorts of incidents abroad, and then it was Pilar's turn to tell her a secret.

"Eduardo doesn't know yet, but I'm going to go into business this year."

"What!" exclaimed her sister-in-law. "What will you do?! How exciting!"

"Well, I've been taking classes, and I'm going to be an interior decorator!"

"No wonder your house is so lovely! You're a natural!"

"I hope so; but I'm going to need help, so Julia is going to assist me, too! She will be paying the Widow Urvina every month for another five years, but it's been her business for a long time."

Eduardo, needing Pilar's attention, called,

"What are you two cooking up already?!'

Pilar smiled at him, with a look of love, not needing to answer.

And Joshua caught Mara's eye, and sent her a silent message, also.

Fifty-eight

At dawn the day following the on-board family dinner, the crew of the *George V* was up and beginning the maneuvers of unloading their ship. The men had had shore leave the night before, and most were still sleepy and yawning as they opened hatches and knotted ropes in the pale light. Both Joshua and Carlo were busy on the Bridge, where the Captain was giving the orders of the day. This trip, his son was going to be in charge of several large deliveries, one of which was to Cecilia Montenegro Granados' store.

By the time the latter shipment was unloaded and piled on the pier, the morning was already hot under a brilliant sun.

Carlo stood on the deck supervising the stacking of the last of the crates, consulting his manifest and looking handsome in his crisp uniform despite the heat and noisy activity around him.

Adalberto Granados had arranged for a truck to pick up the merchandise, and watched it being loaded. The customs officers strolling about the area had already stamped both the goods and the official lists, so they were freed for delivery.

After the area had been emptied and readied for another load of containers to be swung down on cranes from the ship, Carlo came down to the dock, and 'Beto' walked over to shake hands with him before leaving.

"Weren't you here a few years ago? I seem to remember a young guy coming into the store with the Señora Mara and Señora Pilar."

Carlos flashed a smile, saying,

"Of course! Now I remember, too. Aren't you Adalberto Granados? Are you the eldest?"

"Yeah. I'm sort of the head of the family, now."

"Oh, I'm sorry. Did your father pass away?"

"Well, he's not dead, but yes, he *is* 'away'; hasn't been around since I was about thirteen...lives in Manta."

"So your Mom runs the store alone?"

"Yes, but Fernando and I...he's two years younger than I...are trying to get her to ease up a bit. She works too hard-but she's good at it! My sisters aren't much help...they've always been 'too little'!"

"Wow, you have a big family! That's nice. Well, I've got to get back to work; but, officially, I'm in charge of your shipment, so I'll come by the store in a while, to be sure everything is o.k."

The two shook hands, smiling, and agreed to meet later.

The rest of the day passed quickly, as it was always a relief for the men to be able to 'touch ground'; and they actually enjoyed the hard work, knowing their 'reward' would be another night on the town!

Just at sunset, Carlo showered aboard, changed into a fresh uniform and officially began his 'shore leave'! As his father left for the Cottage, where Mara was already installed, he agreed to meet them there later, and headed for "José Montenegro, Hija y Nietos-Importadores'.

Just as he arrived at the store, however, the steel window shutters were being lowered, the metal door cover was pulled down, and all was padlocked.

Fernando Granados was in charge, and greeted him pleasantly.

"Hello there! You must be Juan Carlos. Beto told me you had met this morning."

The two shook hands, and Fernando apologized.

"Sorry we're closed, but all the merchandise has been checked in...everything arrived intact. Thanks for your help with the papers!"

"Well...," began Carlo. "I'll stop by another time to say hello to your mother. I know she's a friend of my Tía Pilar."

"Wait a moment; why don't you come over to the house? It's pretty close, and I know my mother would like to see you. She always speaks fondly of your mother...your family!"

Carlo consulted his watch, then smilingly agreed, since he still had an hour before dinner at Tío Eduardo's.

The two decided to walk, as the sun was setting and the day was cooling in the late afternoon sea breeze.

The Montenegro house was an imposing stucco building; one of the first 'modern' homes built early in the century, in the Spanish style. From the red-tiled roof to the arched gallery with its tiled floors and heavy overhead beams, running all along the outside of the ground floor, it was both inviting and mysterious.

A maid opened the heavy, oversized wooden entrance door as they approached, saying,

"Señor Fernando, your mother was wondering where you were. The cena is ready!"

Fernando glanced at Carlo, and murmured,

"She worries if I'm five minutes late! Come in, and Welcome!"

The whole family was seated in the living room-sala, and Carlo was introduced, shaking hands with them, one by one; first, Cecilia, the mother: still a pretty, plump woman; then Elena, younger than Fernando by two years, the image of her mother! And, after greeting Adalberto again, he turned to the youngest sibling, a girl his age.

"This is Elisa—the baby of the family!" Fernando said fondly. She was his favorite.

"Mucho gusto, how-do-you-do?" said Carlo, taking her hand.

Both he and she looked surprised, for each had felt the shock of static electricity in the hand shake; but it was more than that.

Elisa was obviously the beauty of the family, with thick black curly hair, cut short and framing her lovely face, with its perfectly symmetrical features and naturally rosy cheeks that appeared to have been rouged. Her hazel eyes looked up at him through dark lashes, and she smiled with dimples showing, her long dangle-earrings swinging as she raised her head.

Carlo stood entranced, not releasing her hand.

"Oh, I'm sorry," and their hands parted, eyes still locked.

He couldn't move away; it seemed an eternity, but was only seconds until she looked down and he was released.

Fernando rescued him, saying, "Why don't you stay for supper? We'd be pleased to have you! "

"Of course!" echoed his mother. "Please do stay. It's only a simple meal, I'm afraid."

Carlo, never wanting to leave, said,

"I would like that very much, but Uncle Eduardo is expecting me for dinner with the family tonight."

"Perhaps," suggested Cecilia, "you could telephone him, and maybe join them a little later!"

So that is what he did, agreeing to arrive at the 'Cottage' in time for dessert.

All through the meal at the Montenegro-Granados home, Carlo tried hard to manage his emotions, and carry on polite conversation. But he was seated opposite Elisa, and was incapable of looking away from that adorable face!

She, too, blushed and looked down each time he caught her staring at him.

The time finally came when he could stall no longer, and was forced to keep his word to his uncle. He said goodbye to them all, thanking his hostess for her hospitality, and turned to leave.

Elisa was on the brink of offering to show him out, but the maid, summoned, came in with his cap in hand, and he had no choice but to follow her to the front door.

The minute he was gone, the mother remarked,

"What a nice young man! Too bad he *is* so young!"

Fifty-nine

Five days in port seemed so precious and so fleeting to the Crowley-Castañeda family! So many years to compress into so few hours. So many plans for the future. So many problems to resolve! Mara and Pilar, with their café-con-leches, sat on the Cottage's rear veranda, outside ceiling fans whirring above.

These precious moments had been few, and Mara had bided her time for her revelation to Pilar.

"Pilar, before our dear men appear, I need to tell you something really important!'"

Pilar, sipping her sweet coffee, looked up at her, her lovely hazel eyes softly shining.

"What can that be?"

"Well," said Mara, "about three years ago, in London, I went to see a specialist, a gynecologist; and while there, I asked him some questions about *you*!"

"Me?! In London?! Why?!"

"Well, it has always puzzled me—about the incident leading to Luis' birth! I know it's not my business…but…well…I love you both so much…and Eduardo…and I so much wanted a certain answer from this doctor!"

Pilar, with a pained expression at the old memory, said, "Mara, I want that to be over…forever!"

"I know," insisted her best friend, "but listen! When I gave Dr. Jefferies all the facts, like your having your period the week *before* that terrible act, and the date of your marriage…well…*he* thought…believed…is *sure* that the baby…Luis…is certainly Eduardo's…can *only* be his!"

At this, Pilar began to weep, her emotions so strong, the memories so devastating! All that she had buried for more than twenty years suddenly battered her like the rush of water from a broken dam.

Mara rose and embraced her sobbing friend.

"I love you, Pilar. I so want you—your family—to be completely happy! That's all. Please don't cry! This is *good* news! Please smile for me!"

Pilar looked up, seeing again her dearest friend as a little, laughing golden girl; and now, a caring, precious 'sister'. Her news was all good, just like her Mara!

So she dried her tears, and embraced Mara, saying,

"Oh, is this really true?! My best dream come true?…Thank you, thank you!"

The two sat in harmonious silence, watching the pounding waves as they hit 'their' beach. Both were now tranquil…both now believed this 'new' truth!

****

Carlo was frantic, thinking about his incipient return to England! He had confided to Luis his strong feelings for Elisa, with so little time to see her, let alone to woo her!

And Luis, so full of his…*their* plans, was also frustrated at his best friend-cousin's short stay.

They had been corresponding about their secret plans for more than two years, and now must make a move, or forget them forever!

Carlo, wanting to honor his promises to Luis, but sorely disappointed at having to divide this short time between two such important, life-changing issues, was in an uncharacteristic sour mood.

But Luis had borrowed a friend's old car, and was determined to cheer him up, and 'kidnap' his cousin for the day, at least!

Mara, not knowing what they were up to, had obligingly prepared a picnic basket full of snacks she knew they craved. They thanked her, and embraced her, but wouldn't reveal their plans.

She watched as they disappeared up the street in the old Ford, wondering where they were headed "all day until late."

****

The young men pulled up to the bank in Chone before it had even opened for the day. It was hot and sticky weather, so they headed for a cool bar-restaurant to discuss their next move.

Over soft drinks, Luis informed Carlo of more details; saying that by signing the papers today, and making the down-payment, they would be able to start operations immediately. As soon as they left the bank, he said, the property would be theirs!

They looked at each other, broad grins on their faces, and shook their heads. What a culmination of their dreams!

****

That afternoon, they pushed through the tangle of jungle growth, trying to find the perimeters of their 'new' land. A surveyor had been hired, and would mark it all with stakes; and Luis would supervise the clearing, starting next week.

Everything Carlo would earn in the following two years would go into this secret project! But all in all, the price of the property, now considered a total loss to the bank, was cheap—a 'good buy'!

As soon as the two 'conspirators' returned to Bahía, in the early evening hours, they showered and changed clothing at the Cottage, and Luis accompanied his cousin-best friend to meet the cause of Carlo's now-buoyant spirits.

When the handsome young men knocked on the heavy door of the Montenegro-Granados home, it was opened by Elena. Luis looked questioningly at Carlo, who shook his head imperceptibly.

The older daughter smiled knowingly, and led them both to the sala, where they waited, standing, for her to call her sister.

When Elisa entered the room and saw the two men together, she was startled, thinking them twins! But Carlo stepped forward and took her hand—again—and she looked frankly and happily into his blue eyes. She was won without a battle!

Carlo received this silent message with his heart almost bursting with love and thankfulness.

He then regained his composure, introduced Luis, and the three sat together on a large couch.

"Señorita Granados," began Carlo. "May I say 'Elisa'?! "

She nodded, smiling, and he continued,

"I think I can speak frankly in front of my cousin…he's like a brother to me!…Elisa…May I call on you while I'm in port? I only have a few days!"

He looked at her imploringly, knowing he had only four days of this Heaven left!

"Well," replied Elisa, "in spite of your 'brother's' presence, I think I can say…frankly…yes, I'd enjoy getting to know you. In fact, I feel I already do!"

"May I hold your hand…just a moment?" asked Carlo, emboldened by such a positive answer.

She smiled broadly then, a mischievous twinkle in her eyes, her dimple beckoning him, and silently put out her small hand.

Luis, knowing something serious was progressing here, cleared his throat and rose.

"Please excuse me, Señorita Elisa, but I have delivered my cousin safely, and now I must keep an appointment of my own." And he edged toward the door.

Before Elisa or Carlo could say a word, he was gone, and the señorita's small hand was engulfed by the Third Officer's large one.

They sat there together in silence for a long moment. Then, at the same instant, they leaned toward each other, two magnets drawing irrevocably together. She tilted her face up to his, and their lips met softly together.

But Carlo could not pass this first test! He dropped her hand and folded her to his chest, his arms tightly around her, and their lips met once more in a passionate kiss.

At this moment, the hall door opened, and Elisa's mother entered the room.

"¡Dios mío!" she cried. "What is going on here? Elisa…what behavior! With a boy you just met!"

Elisa knew Cecilia well. She understood that she would always be the 'baby' in her eyes...that her mother wanted to keep her 'pet' as long as possible.

"Mamá," she announced. "Juan Carlos is *not* a 'boy'...nor am I a 'girl'! we're both of age...and we are not doing anything disgraceful...We love each other, that's all!"

Carlo was more dumbfounded than Cecilia...hearing his new-found beloved defending him and declaring her love, both to her parent and to him!

Was there ever a luckier man?!

****

The poor mother, defenseless against her 'baby' daughter was now assaulted on three fronts at once...

As Luis was leaving, he met Elena once more, and sparks flew between them, as well!

"You're leaving so soon?" she had asked in surprise.

"Yes...but...well...I don't suppose you'd like to leave with me?...that is...well, I thought maybe we could get acquainted on a little walk?"

She studied the honest face of this good-looking man, whom she had admired from the first introduction.

She was not a beauty, but, like her mother, had a pretty face, and was more 'rounded' than her slim younger sister. She had always been 'The Smart One', 'The Adviser', 'The Reliable One', so many young men had been rather wary of her, not seeing her soft, very feminine interior.

But Luis saw it at once, felt it, wanted to know more about it!

"Yes," she answered. "I'd like that very much...just let me get my hat. Wait here, please."

She returned a moment later with a wide straw hat. She had a soft sprinkling of freckles across her nose, making her pale face, with its big warm eyes, seem girlish.

Luis thought her very appealing, and escorted her out to the street.

At that very moment, a man, wearing formal, rather rumpled out-of-date clothing was approaching the house. He stopped in his tracks when he saw them, then continued up to the heavy front door without speaking.

"Hurry," Elena said softly, turning her head away from the man. And they quickened their steps, going around the corner and towards the nearby beachfront.

"That was my father!" she said softly. "We rarely see him, and have nothing to do with him anymore…he deserted us…long ago, you know."

"That's Alberto Granados?!" exclaimed Luis in surprise. "I've heard stories about him, but didn't really believe them!"

"Well, they were probably true. He's become stranger and stranger as the years go by! He's probably come to ask Mother for money!"

Luis, anxious to talk about '*her*' or '*them*! gently pulled her along, until they came to a small park, and he guided her to a shady jacaranda tree with a bench beneath it.

He, too, was anxious to hold her hand, while hearing her sweet voice tell him all about herself. This was not a problem, as she willingly held his hand, and told him stories about her growing up with an affectionate family.

And he confided things to her that only Carlo had learned through his letters.

Both felt they had wasted time not getting to know each other before, despite living in the same small city, only blocks apart!

But both were equally determined to rectify this situation immediately. Starting this evening, Luis invited her to meet his parents before seeing a movie. Then they made plans for days and weeks ahead!

Luis thought fleetingly of Carlo, knowing he, too, was going to see more of Elisa.

Truly, their paths were meant to meet!

Sixty

Elena had been correct in assuming that her father was after money! But, besides this, he had left threatening warnings in his wake. He had seen a 'Castañeda' in Luis' face, and was doubly infuriated when he heard that Carlo, too, had come calling!

"I will wait outside and kill any member of that—family who dares to sully ours!" he had raged.

Cecilia, who had just delivered a monetary ultimatum of her own, said coldly,

"There is no 'ours', you pompous—! And hasn't been for many years! Besides not "sharing" in the rewards of *our* hard work, you won't share in this home, from my *father's* hard work, and you have *nothing* to say about whom my daughters see—or love—or marry!!"

At last, Alberto had left, a defeated man. But his rancor ran deep, and he was determined to follow the easiest path left to him. After all, how difficult would it be to shoot such easy targets?! He headed for his lodgings here in Bahía, where he had stashed his gun.

Cecilia, though, was far more worried than she had appeared to her 'husband'! For years, he had seemed unbalanced: irrationally angry and revengeful by turns; and today, he seemed to have gone over the edge!

She went to the living room, where Elisa and Carlo sat talking softly, hand in hand, a worried frown on her face.

"Perdónenme! Excuse me—Elisa, your father was just here, and Juan Carlos, he's in an irrational rage about the Castañedas coming here! and I'm very worried.!"

"Excuse me, Señora...but I'm just *one* Castañeda...you said more?"

"Oh," she answered, suddenly flopping down into a big chair.

"I'm really upset! Can you get me a glass of cold water, Mijita?"

Elisa rose at once, a worried expression on her now serious face; her mother was not prone to histrionics. She kissed her first, then ran out of the room to get a drink for her, returning quickly.

"Señora, why are you so worried? Tell me, please!"

So she recounted what had happened between her husband and herself, and told Carlo that Alberto had seen Luis leave the house with Elena, who had not even greeted her father.

At this, Carlo was totally alert, and volunteered to call the police at once.

"Do you know where he's staying? I know he doesn't live here in Bahía anymore."

She wasn't sure, but thought he might be at a cousin's and gave him the address, which Carlo passed on to the policeman on the line.

Carlo stayed with the women, torn between protecting them, and finding Luis, who might be in grave danger!

He looked out the window, and saw a police car pulling up to the curb, so he excused himself and went to the entrance door.

A young police officer was coming up the walk with Luis and Elena.

"Thanks for your description, sir. They were easy to spot."

He spoke deferentially, impressed with Carlo's uniform.

"We have that address covered, and are on the lookout for the man in your report. They told us at the house that he's carrying a weapon. I'll return later, if necessary, sir." And he got back into his Chevrolet to continue the search.

Carlo called the Cottage to let them know what had happened, and asked his mother to "keep Tío Eduardo indoors with them." He and Luis would wait at the Granados home until the police advised them that it was safe to leave.

The few hours that then passed in Cecilia's home were all that were needed for several lives to change forever. No more time was necessary for the two young couples to know that they needed each other and wanted to be together for the rest of their time on earth!

By nightfall, the two young women knew of the 'secret plan', to remain a sacred trust among the four, though it meant that Elisa would have to wait two years to have Carlo near her forever!

And Cecilia, upon hearing only part of these precipitous intentions, decided that Youth was in the right this time; agreeing that it was better to help them marry now.

Her sons, too, saw that their sisters had found true love with excellent men, whom they would be proud to call brothers!

In another hour, the day's alert was over and Alberto Granados was in the hands of the police. He had been in a frenzy when they found him, waving the pistol and swearing vengeance on the Castañeda family! For the moment, he was locked up; but no one was sure what to do with him! A doctor had examined him and, not being a specialist, had advised sending the prisoner to Quito, to a special mental hospital, for possible treatment there.

****

The plans for the double wedding went forward quickly, and, with Joshua and Mara's blessing, as well as Pilar and Eduardo's, the date was set for the day before the *George V* was to sail!

Everyone in the surrounding family celebrated the romantic weddings! All the aunts, uncles, cousins and friends were alerted and happily united in a hurry, to see the young men and their pretty brides begin their lives together.

But no one, except the four celebrated ones, knew of the secret future they were to have! And so it remained—a secret—for the next two years!

****

When the *George V* sailed, its Third Officer was a proud-happy/ sad husband! Carlo waved and blew kisses to his adorable new wife as the ship pulled slowly out to sea. Only the 'Plan' sustained him, as the terrible emptiness without her made Carlo feel slightly seasick for the first time!

But his cousin/brother, on shore between the two sisters, bolstered his spirits in his unhappiness. He knew that those three partners of 'the plan' would keep their promises and make the future of his dreams a reality.

On board, Mara blew a kiss to Joshua, standing on the Bridge: her knight—so handsome—so loving and good! Then, she covered her tearful son's hand with hers, as they stood at the railing, no longer able to distinguish the tiny dots along the shore.

EPILOGUE

*1938*The recently commissioned *King George VI* eased into the
Bahía harbor in May, 1938, with two new officers aboard: The captain,
a Mark Herrington, and the Second Mate, Juan Carlos Castañeda-
Crowley, with his understudy, soon to take his place, Benjamin
Oakley.

Besides the crew, the ship brought ret. Captain Joshua Crowley,
his wife Mara, and all their baggage and belongings.

They were met at the dock by the requested van. As soon as their
possessions passed customs inspection, they were loaded into it.
Surrounded by family and friends, they headed for the Cottage.

Carlo wanted only one thing, and there she was, more beautiful
than before! All the way 'home' to Uncle Eduardo's, Carlo held Elisa
in his arms. He promised never to leave her again; and she, her long
waiting over, never ever wanted to be out of this circle of warmth and
security!

All her letters had proclaimed her love and sadness at their
separation. But she had been almost too busy to worry. She, Luis and
Elena had been going over architects' plans for over a year; and,
before that, were weeks spent in Chone, for meetings with Alfonso,
who was their mentor and guide for the new life they were to build.

Now, just in time to give Carlo a welcome surprise, they were
ready for his inspection.

****

Pilar and Eduardo had had their own 'secret'. They had been

enlarging and renovating Joshua's house on Marbella Street for two years; and Pilar had done the interior decorating in a style she hoped Mara would like.

Now, the little white house was a tall home, with graceful trees shading its garden. On its roof was a watch-tower, with an unobstructed view far out to sea. Its two storeys had wide, shuttered balconies, and the interior rooms had been completely modernized. Outside its gate an iron sign read 'Casa Crowley'!

Mara and Joshua were enchanted with the surprise of a home of their own: a place for a perpetual honeymoon!

Now they could unload the moving van, and settle down to the peaceful life they had dreamed of for so long!

****

Both Pilar and Eduardo had long been guessing about the almost daily trips Luis and Elena were making.

The two newlyweds had moved in with his parents, since the house had so much unused space now. Their life there, though blissfully happy, had been saddened by Carlo's leaving.

Elisa had stayed on at her mother's, but joined her sister and new brother-in-law daily, to work with them on the 'plan'.

In two years, Elisa had grown to be a responsible woman, loyal to her absent husband, and a true partner in the work toward his goal...

The first weekend after the ship's arrival, the four young people invited both Luis' and Carlo's parents, and Doña Cecilia to come and witness a surprise!

Two cars-full made the once-long trip to Chone in under an hour, though the road was unpaved and bumpy.

Where there hadn't been more than a trail for many years, there was now a narrow road, and a bridge crossing a deep gorge, so that they could drive all the way to the 'project' from Chone.

Suddenly they stopped at a gate, where an iron sign swung from new posts.

Eduardo stared unbelievingly at it, tears in his eyes.

"PARAISO"

Luis jumped out to unlock the gate, and the cars followed a now-smoother, wider road that wound through the tall trees to the very spot of the 'old' compound.

But now the houses were very different from the home Eduardo had known. The twin houses were long and low; they were of white stucco, with thick walls and tiled roofs, air-conditioning units in most of the deep-set, shuttered windows. Each had a wide, tile-floored covered porch, and new vines were already blooming up their sides. The tidy lawn and flower beds softened the landscape under numerous shady fruit trees.

But gone were the shed and drying racks, and the old worker-housing.

Far back, away from the two homes, was a shady street with single stucco cottages along it, and gates to the new product of Paraiso: kilometer after kilometer of banana trees grew in orderly profusion!

Mara turned to Carlo; love, pride and surprise in her question. "Did you know about this, Mijito?! Is this then the secret you kept so well?!"

Then they explained that Tío Alfonso had been their guide from the first, teaching them all he knew of banana cultivation. It was he who had planned, purchased and directed the building of the necessary equipment for mass production and export, so that they could by-pass the usual middleman, and have a far more profitable operation.

Alfonso had directed the erection of their funicular, which, on its steel cable would bring the hooked branches of fruit sliding down to the preservation-wash tubs. Then the branches would be fumigated and sealed into ticketed, airtight bags for shipping in forty-three-pound boxes.

For this tremendous effort, the young group of owners had made him an active partner for life!

And he was here today, smiling and embracing his sister and all the family.

****

Ecuador was becoming the world's largest exporter of bananas; and, though the future would perhaps bring more competition, it was the country's primary source of income for many years.

Carlo and Luis became very prosperous, and, once more, Paraiso was blessed with the love and attention that had made it thrive under their fathers' care.

Again, there were happy families living inside the ring of jungle all around them.

Luis and Elena had their child first; a dark-haired, green-eyed boy...the image of his Grandma Pilar: 'Carlos Eduardo.'

Carlo and Elisa followed them with a precious little blonde girl, Elisa Margarita.

Mara and Joshua, living in their 'new' house by the sea, were frequent visitors, along with Pilar and Eduardo.

Cecilia often drove out with them so they could all enjoy their grandchildren together.

And, luckily for the 'new' men of Paraiso, Pepín, their neighbor, helped them as he had helped their fathers.

Once again, Paraiso was truly a Paradise.

The End

Printed in the United States
50139LVS00002B/481